On the Sidelines

Full of Running #1

on the sidelines

GRACE WILKINSON

First edition

Also by the author

Comet in Summer

Confetti Horses

Eventing Bay

The Loxwood Series

chapter 1

'See, isn't this a nice place?'

Yes, I think, standing in the yard, but I'm not going to say it. Not yet, anyway. Sixteen stables built of dark wood, with white painted doors, run around a courtyard, and although it isn't the smartest yard in Suffolk, there's something homely about it. Luckily for me, Jupiter whinnies in the trailer, saving me from voicing my thoughts, and I merely shrug in reply as I set about unbolting the ramp.

'Leave him a sec, Sybs,' Mum says. 'Let's check with Rose first before unloading him.' She steps in front of the car, looking to the left. 'Can you see, she's teaching another lesson right now. Isn't that a nice horse?'

You'd think *nice* were the only word my mum knows. Everything's nice lately. The new café she's going to run, the cottage we visited earlier this week, this yard she wants me to move my pony to, and last but not least, the person who runs it, an event rider called Rose Holloway.

'She's so lovely, Sybil,' Mum said at dinner two nights ago. My brother and I had been dragged to the cottage

Mum wants to rent the day before, which wasn't so bad, and one of the better changes going on in my life, but somehow, amidst the divorce and house move drama, it hadn't occurred to me that I would have to move livery yards, too.

'I'm sure she is,' I replied, still reeling from Mum's announcement that she'd been to visit a yard down the road from where we would be moving, 'but I like how things are. Why would I want to leave Eva's?'

'Why would you keep Jupiter in a yard in Cambridge when you could have him just down the lane? And the woman who runs it, Rose, is a professional event rider - she rode to three-star level. I thought this would be a no-brainer for you.'

'Eva's ridden to one-star,' I said, but my mind was whirling with the thought of training with an Advanced event rider. Still, I didn't want to leave the yard I knew better than home.

'You're really going to like Rose,' Mum went on. 'She's just so nice.'

'What's wrong with Eva?'

'Nothing's wrong with Eva. But Rose is... softer. I don't know, she just felt more approachable. She's a mum, too.'

'Being a mum doesn't mean anything,' I snapped. 'That's not a reason to like somebody.'

'Her daughters ride,' Mum said.

'Even worse. She's probably one of those pushy parents who's too busy training her kids to win to teach other people.'

'She's not like that, Sybil.'

'You only spoke to her for two minutes!'

'Just try it,' Mum said quickly. 'One lesson. She said you could go Saturday afternoon, so we'll trailer Jupiter over and you can just see for yourself.'

I looked down at my plate, spearing a piece of broccoli with my fork. 'And if I don't like it?'

Mum let out a long breath. 'If you don't like it, then you can keep Jupiter at Eva's, figure out a way to pay for part livery, and accept that you might not see as much of him.'

And that was the last we said of it. I went to the yard as usual this morning, where, much to my annoyance, Eva was in a particularly tricky mood, complaining about what a mess the place was and leaving me with no time to talk with her, to ask for some advice before going for a lesson with somebody else, talk about what Jupiter needs, because my biggest fear is that I'll be asked to do something neither of us is capable of, but it didn't happen. So I got my pony ready, loaded his tack into the tack compartment of the trailer, and now here we are.

'Look, Sybil,' Mum says, resting her hands on her hips as she watches the horse in the ring. 'That looks good.'

I walk up beside Mum, the sun in my eyes as I squint to see the figures in the sand school. A chestnut horse is cantering around a line of fences that is set down the middle of the ring, and to one side of the jumps stands who I assume is Rose. I can't really see her face from a distance, but she's of average height, with a typical rider's build, and dark hair in a ponytail. Even though she isn't riding, she is clad in boots and chaps.

'And again,' Rose calls to the rider. 'Don't rush him on the approach to the first, but make sure you keep moving for the two strides to the second, and sit up for the third.' She looks towards us now, as the rider sets her horse up on a circle, and waves. Even though I can't make out her features, I can see Rose smile from here. 'Hi! Sorry I'm running a bit late.'

'Oh, no problem, we're early,' Mum calls. We aren't early, but whatever.

'I'll be five more minutes if you want to watch or start getting ready. And there's a kettle in the tack room if you want a tea or coffee.'

'We're fine,' Mum says, and just when I want to ask her to help me tack up, she starts striding towards the sand school, so I follow. 'Isn't this school a good size?' she goes on, speaking quietly. 'And I like the sand surface so much more than that rubber stuff Eva has.' I turn to the side and cross my arms, blanking her, and watch the ring.

The chestnut is cantering towards the grid, staying round through the turn to the first fence. He's a real sport horse-type, with a high neck carriage and well-muscled haunches. I don't think the rider's that great as I get a first glimpse of her up close, her position a bit scruffy on the approach to the first obstacle, but the horse has a scopey jump, knees tucked, and comes alive when he lands on the other side of the jump, looking like a harder ride than he did a moment ago. He has Thoroughbred in him, I think as he goes on to the second fence, energetic, but the rider seems to know how to keep him right, how he needs to be ridden, and they clear the fence, landing a tad far out, and she has to shorten the chestnut to meet the next one-stride distance, and the horse jumps enormously over the metre-ten upright. She's maybe not the most polished rider, but she must be used to all sorts of horses because she barely moves in the saddle, and not only that, but she makes the awkward stride and big jump look all right.

The horse tucks his nose to his chest on landing, and his rider pushes a hand forward to touch him on the neck -

only a touch, not a pat.

'Good girl,' Rose calls. 'You did really well to keep him straight through that line, and you didn't let anything fluster you. You had an awkward distance because he jumped so far out, but you made the best of it. Just do it one more time, and then if that's okay we'll leave him on that for today.'

The rider nods, and I try to get a look at her face, but fail. How much older than me is she? A lot, I hope. Yes, she must be. Okay. It's normal that she rides better than me. She's older. I'm sure I'll ride that well when I'm her age, too. Just because everyone else I know is already moving up to Novice -

'Sybil.' Mum's voice cuts into my internal rambling. 'Why don't you go get Jupiter ready?'

'Hi, Sybil,' Rose says from behind her. She's still smiling, and up close she looks younger than I expected. Early thirties? She must be, if she has kids old enough to ride, but I wouldn't think anything of somebody saying she's twenty. Maybe she's the same age as Mum but just doesn't look it. 'It's nice to meet you.'

'You too,' I mumble, because polite responses come out of my mouth even when I don't want them to.

'You going to go get Jupi ready, Sybs,' Mum says again, and I clench my teeth at her words. She knows I hate it when she calls me *Sybs* in public, and I was also hoping she'd help me get ready.

I step back. 'Fine.' Too late I realise I don't know what I'm doing, whether Rose expects me to do flatwork or jump, but I've already turned away, and I don't want to go back. Besides, Mum and Rose already seem to be chatting, and that's not something I want to be part of.

There's another trailer next to ours, attached to an old

Jeep - presumably belonging to the girl in the lesson. She mustn't be a livery client, then.

'Hey, Jup,' I say, lowering the ramp. It's his ears I see first, the grey tips, followed by a curious-looking head, held high, and the pink snip on his nose. My pony stands with his chest pushed against the breast bar keeping him in the trailer stall, a half-empty haynet hanging in front of him. The speed at which he eats, even in stressful situations, could win him awards. And it would be the first thing he's ever won.

'What do you think?' I ask him. In response, Jupiter lets out another whinny, his awful, high-pitched whinny, and is met with a couple of responses from horses in the yard, as well as the chestnut in the sand school, who neighs even though he's cantering. 'Look what you've done,' I snap. The last thing I need is for my horse to ruin somebody else's lesson. If that happened, I really would never come back here again. But the chestnut loses interest quickly, resuming his rhythm.

I tie Jupiter to the side of the trailer and start unwrapping his bandages, but he's being a pain, moving from one side to the other, pinning himself against the trailer to turn his head and look at the other horses. If only I had travel boots, like every other equestrian in the twenty-first century, but it's a cost I have yet to justify. But somehow, amidst Jupiter's prancing, I manage to get the bandages off, chucking them into the trailer, and I pull his gear out of the tack compartment. The saddle isn't mine, belongs to Jupiter and goes where he goes, was loaned out with him to the rider he went to before me, too. It's old, and not as comfortable as those my friends ride in, but it's a perfect fit. I lay the navy blue saddle cloth on his back, unclip the rope from his head collar to slide the breastplate over his head, deciding to have his jumping gear on just in case, clip it back on again, and grab the saddle and the girth. It's a squeeze at the best of times, but today Jupiter is blowing out his stomach for all he's worth, and my fingers are numb by the time I manage to hook the girth a hole. I know it'll go up another four in a minute, once the stubborn pony gives up the act, not that he isn't still chubby.

Jupiter whinnies again while I'm putting on his tendon boots, and I look up to see the chestnut horse from the school walking over on a long rein, the rider's feet out of the stirrups. This time, the chestnut doesn't whinny in response. I never know if I should say hello or resume my activity in situations like this, but the girl smiles, so I smile back. Yes, definitely older than me. Maybe not even in her teens. At least Rose won't be expecting me to ride to the same standard.

'Sorry about him,' I say, nodding at Jupiter, who is straining against the rope for no purpose other than to make my life difficult.

She shakes her head, sliding off the horse as they reach the trailer beside me. 'Oh, no, don't worry about it. Lox doesn't care. Do you?' She says that last part to her horse, grinning as he turns to look at her, and she plants a kiss on his wide forehead. For all of his qualities, Jupiter would leap backwards if I tried doing that to him. 'He's a cutie,' the girl says, talking to me again as she inclines her head towards Jup.

'Looks can be deceiving,' I say, which makes her laugh, and I feel myself warm to her.

'How're you doing, Sybil?' comes Mum's voice as she and Rose walk up to us. 'You not ready?'

'Sorry, my fault,' the girl with the chestnut says quickly,

leading her horse to the head collar hanging from her trailer, which isn't true because I haven't stopped fastening tendon boots in the twenty seconds she's been here, but I'm sure Mum knows that.

'Don't worry, there's no rush,' Rose says. 'All mine are already worked, and none of the liveries are using the school today. Or at all, really. Everyone here's a happy hacker at the moment, so it's mostly just me, and even my horses hack half the week.'

Whether or not Rose knows it I don't know, but she's just dangled a carrot in front of me. At Eva's, a livery yard of twenty horses, each owner more arrogant and competitive than the next, time in the sand school is more precious than gold dust. On weekends especially, I'm lucky if I can have fifteen minutes in it, and have had to accept that I won't be able to ride and just go home on multiple occasions. Hacking isn't the best there, either, and I get nervous taking Jupiter out alone anyway.

'What a lovely horse,' Mum says, approaching the chestnut. She holds out a hand, placing it on his neck at the girl's nod of consent. 'Hey, beautiful. How old is he? What's his name?'

'Loxwood,' the girl replies. 'He's six.'

'He's lovely. Isn't he lovely, Sybil?'

I nod briefly, wishing Mum would stop making such a show about everything in this yard - the sand school, the horses, the people - being so nice and lovely.

'I still can't get over all the horses around here,' Mum goes on. 'I was in Newmarket at eight in the morning the other day, and they're everywhere. Racehorses walking the streets! How many are there?'

'Three thousand,' the girl says. 'Three thousand in the

town, same number again in the studs.'

'It's amazing,' Rose says. 'And the best part is that you can go out like this' - she gestures at her jodhpurs and boots - 'without being stared at.'

The girl nods. 'You'd stand out if you *didn't.*'

'We're easily pleased,' Rose laughs. 'But it is a great place to live, especially with horses even if you're not involved with racing. Abundance of farriers, feed suppliers, some of the best equine hospitals in the world right on our doorstep...'

'It's such a multicultural town, too, thanks to the racing,' says the girl.

Mum grins at me. 'Well, we're very much looking forward to it.'

'And am I remembering right that you said you're opening a café in town?' Rose asks.

'Yes, that's right,' Mum says. 'I used to work in catering before the kids, and the person who owns the place is a friend of mine, and when the manager she hired dropped out a few weeks ago, she asked if I'd be interested, and that was that. We open in two weeks, and I really want it to just be a nice, friendly place anyone can go.' *Isn't that what all cafés are,* I think.

'That sounds great! I'm sure it'll be a hit in the morning with exercise riders,' says Rose. We drove through Newmarket this afternoon, seeing the slightly rundown high street, and it looked to me that the last thing the town needs is another coffee shop. 'Does it have a name?'

I look at Mum, who also looks at me, then down at my feet. 'Yes,' she says tentatively. 'Sybil's not that keen, I know, but my friend and I wanted something that linked to horses and racing, to embody the town's culture, and we thought of

The Home Stretch Café.'

'Oh, I love that!'

'Me too,' the girl says. 'It's clever, because like you say it makes you think of racing, but then the word *home* also gives it a friendly feel...'

'Exactly! I know *Home Straight* would be more British, but it just doesn't sound right... I'm glad you like it. Both of you call by anytime once we open and coffee and cake's on me.'

'Speaking of, are you sure I can't get you a drink?' Rose asks. 'Tea? Coffee?'

Mum shakes her head. 'I'm fine, thanks. Maybe later.'

'Sybil?'

'No, thank you,' I mumble, unbuckling Jupiter's reins to slide them through the martingale, fastening the buckle before passing them over his head.

'Aren't you a cutie?' Rose goes on, coming up to Jupiter. Because he thinks everyone in the world lives to worship and feed him, Jupiter takes a step forward, away from me, to reach Rose, and she laughs. 'Hey, naughty. Don't do that, you'll get me in trouble with your mum.' She pushes his chest to make him take a step back, and I hold on to Jupi's head with my right hand, unbuckling the head collar to pull the bridle on, passing his ears beneath the headpiece.

'He's cheeky,' Mum says.

'He's a lovely little thing,' Rose says. She looks at him a moment before turning back to Mum. 'You know, I can't help but think we've met before. It's been bugging me all week.'

'Really? At an event, maybe? Sybil's been competing BE for a year.'

'No, I don't think so, I'd remember. I feel like it was a

long time ago. You said you're from the area? Did *you* ever ride?'

Mum perks up. 'When I was Sybil's age, but only Pony Club.'

Rose nods slowly. 'That rings a bell. Did you say your name's Maya?'

'I rode a chestnut cob-like pony,' Mum offers. She frowns. 'See, now you mention it, you do look familiar, too. Rose Holloway,' she mumbles to herself.

'Holloway's my married name,' Rose says. 'I was Rose Mackenzie.'

The name sparks Mum's memory, and she's snapping her fingers. 'Yes, I remember! You used to wear your hair in plaits and you rode a bay-'

'Yes!' Rose laughs. 'Oh my god, it's such a small world.'

'The horse world is,' Mum says.

'Sounds like fate,' the girl with the chestnut says behind me, which is not at all helpful. I don't want to come here, no matter how nice Rose is.

'So, do you still ride?'

'Oh, no,' Mum replies, shaking her head. 'Life got in the way. I just get my horse fix with Sybil, looking after Jupi while she's at school.'

'You're the sensible one. How about you, Sybil?' Rose looks at me. 'Are you riding for pleasure or wanting to make a career out of it?'

'For pleasure,' I say. 'I'm not good enough to ride professionally, and working with horses full-time seems like too much work, anyway.' Rose laughs, as does the girl behind me, and their eyes meet as they grin again.

'Smart move,' the girl says.

Rose nods. 'I think I actually spend less time with

horses working with them full-time than I did when I was just riding for fun. Georgia?'

The girl - Georgia - nods too, stepping beside me, her horse tied to the trailer, already untacked in the time we've been talking. She still has her riding hat on, messy hair tied at the nape of her neck, and her T-shirt reveals the kind of strong arms all riders have. 'Yep. That definitely sounds about right.'

'Better for me,' Mum says. 'The amount some of these people spend...' She shakes her head in disbelief. 'Sybil's got a couple of friends who ride FEI ponies, and the price tags on them - I actually can't get my head around it. Sybil's best friend, Freya, lives just down the road from here, actually.'

'Really?' Rose smiles. 'Whereabouts?'

'Half a mile down this lane - the chocolate-box thatch on the corner.'

'With that lovely big willow tree?' says Rose. 'Oh, how great! You could go riding together.' *Don't remind me,* I think. Of course moving to the outskirts of Newmarket, to one of the picturesque English county villages where everybody seems to have horses and stables, with my pony within walking distance, and being able to go for rides with my best friend has always been a dream. But I never thought it would really happen, and if it did it was supposed to be with Mum *and* Dad, not under these circumstances...

'She hasn't got a new pony yet, though,' I point out. Freya sold her first pony last month, as her parents decided to start looking for a potential European ride.

'Hasn't she bought an FEI pony now?' Mum insists, turning back to Rose. 'They're getting a pony that won a team medal at Europeans some years ago. What's his name, Sybil? Ba-'

'You're not supposed to say anything,' I snap, cutting Mum off before she can speak the name. 'It's a secret, until the Pony long list is announced.' I know how rude it is of me to leave Rose and Georgia out of the conversation like that, but it's true. There isn't exactly an abundance of FEI event ponies, and the politics involved make real politics look like child's play. 'They won't be buying him if he makes the European team,' I say instead, covering for myself. 'They wouldn't be able to afford him.'

'They can't afford him anyway,' Mum says, addressing Rose and Georgia. 'They're scraping together every penny they have to get Freya a pony to do Europeans on.'

'Freya rides really well,' I say in my friend's defence. 'And they think she could go pro, so they're just trying to do everything they can to help.'

Mum nods. 'Lovely pony,' she goes on. 'Though I'm a sucker for a chestnut. And luckily for Nell and Craig' - Freya's parents - 'he hasn't made a team with his next rider, otherwise the price would be double or triple what it is.'

'The pony market is mad,' Rose agrees.

'Wait a second,' Georgia says, wearing the face of someone who's just cracked a code. 'Are you talking about Battersea?'

My stomach sinks, and I glare at Mum. She just *had* to go and blab. They aren't so many ponies on the circuit that a rider can't guess which one is in question from only minor details. Of course there's only one chestnut FEI pony coming up for sale whose name starts with the syllable *Ba*.

'Yes, that's it!' Mum says happily, and then seeing my expression she adds to me, 'It's not like they're going to tell anyone, Sybil.'

'No, no, of course not,' Rose says.

Georgia shakes her head. 'I won't say a thing. His stable name's Leo, right? It's just that the person who used to ride him, who took him to Europeans, is a really close friend of mine.'

'No way!' Mum looks excitedly at us all in turn. 'Well, this really *is* a small world.'

'Too small,' I mutter under my breath.

I don't think Mum hears. 'So your daughters ride too,' she goes on, talking to Rose. 'Do they event?'

'Goodness, no.' Rose laughs. 'I'm trying to avoid that if I can. I've managed to keep them out of Pony Club this long, at least. They each have a pony to muck around on, but I'm hoping horses will just be a phase. My oldest, Mackenzie, is more interested, and I let her do little unaffiliated shows to satisfy her, but unfortunately she's quite keen. Jemima's less interested, only really enjoys plodding around, so I think I'm all right there, but Kenzie... I'm dreading the year she turns twelve and starts asking to event affiliated.'

'Good luck,' Georgia says with a grin.

'Mackenzie's quite a character,' Rose says to us. 'She and Jemima are the same height now, so the easiest way to tell them apart is to think that Kenzie never shuts up, and Mima never speaks.'

I laugh despite myself. Here I was prepared for some arrogant, pushy event mum, and Rose is the opposite. Some good news, at least.

'How old are they?' Mum asks.

'Um. Ten and eight, I think.' Rose frowns, then laughs again. 'Yeah, that must be right.' She shakes her head. 'Ask me any of the horses' birth dates, but my kids'...'

Okay, maybe I *could* grow to like her.

'Anyway.' She taps her hands against her legs. 'I'll stop boring you, and focus on *you.*' Rose speaks this last word to Jupiter, leaning forward to scratch his head. My pony stretches his neck out, enjoying the attention, and I smile. I don't think Eva has ever touched him other than to adjust tack, let alone addressed him directly.

'I need to get going, too,' Georgia says. 'I have to meet my parents for dinner later.'

'Say hi for me,' Rose says.

'Will do.'

'Nice to meet you,' Mum says.

'You too.' She smiles at me. 'Have a nice ride.'

As Georgia speedily loads her horse onto the trailer and climbs into the jeep, Mum says to Rose, 'What a nice girl.'

'Isn't she?' Rose says. 'Hard worker, too. Right.' She looks at me. 'Ready to go?'

Jupiter is spicy when we walk into the school, but that's nothing out of the ordinary. He's a quiet ride at home, but when he goes to a show he comes alive. It's also the reason I've never not been nearly last after dressage.

'So just spend ten minutes warming him up as you would at home,' Rose calls to me as she walks to the centre of the sand school. I thought she'd stay with Mum at the railings, but she's switched to coach mode. 'I won't say anything, just let you do what you would normally, because you know your pony better than I do. Okay?'

I nod, looking straight ahead as I shorten my reins. It feels so weird, being in a lesson with somebody else. Not Eva's arena, not Eva's voice in the centre of the circle, not the same expectations.

'Okay,' Rose repeats. 'So, while you're walking, why

don't you tell me about your pony and what you've achieved up to now - and what you wish to.'

I relax, conversation saving me from the unbearable silence of scrutiny. 'I've had him a year and a half,' I begin. 'I got him on loan from somebody who competed up to BE100, which is what his first rider did with him too, and we completed two BE90s last year, and one this year which we placed at.' I pause. Funny how quickly everything can be summed up. 'He's twelve, so he's still young enough to make it to Novice. He's not the best at flatwork and he loves jumping but I find it hard to control him.'

'Gets strong?'

'Yeah. And he lifts his head, so I always jump him with a martingale.'

'And your goal is to get him to Novice?'

'I'd like to do a pony one-star,' I say, my voice shaking as I speak the words. 'It's probably not possible, but I'd like to just achieve one.' I've voiced this to Eva before, in spurts of bravery, but never really had the response I was hoping for.

'You're thirteen this year?' Rose asks.

I nod. 'I was thirteen in March.'

'Oh, well there's no reason that shouldn't be possible, then.'

Her enthusiasm surprises me, and I bite my lip to stop from smiling. 'Really?'

'Of course! You've got three years yet. Plenty of time. You said he likes jumping, that's all you need. Good attitude. The rest can be taught. There's no reason you can't make it.'

My mind is buzzing thanks to Rose's words as I warm Jupiter up, hoping I can convince her she's right. Jupiter is fresh, revving to go, which makes my job a lot easier. I trot him on a twenty-metre circle, changing direction every so often, trying to get him moving forward and flexing to the inside. Rose goes to stand beside Mum while I'm going around, her eyes staying on Jupiter and me even as they chat, and the suspense makes my stomach flip. Does she think we look all right? Does she think I can ride? I think Jupiter feels good, but I have no idea if Rose thinks the same.

Finally, after five minutes of me trotting, she walks back to the centre of the school and calls, 'Okay, come back to a walk when you're ready.'

I close my fingers on the reins, sitting in the saddle, and gradually Jupi comes to a walk. His head comes up, neck tense, but I let out the reins and he lowers his head again.

'How was that transition?'

'Sorry?' I didn't hear the words at first, though they've now settled in my mind, and I can't understand the meaning.

'The transition,' Rose says again, crossing her arms to walk alongside me and Jupiter, swinging from one foot to the other to stay level with us. 'When you came back to a walk.'

'Uh.' I didn't think about the transition, just brought Jupiter back to a walk. What does she mean? 'I didn't know I had to think about the transition.'

'You didn't know you had to think about it?' Rose repeats, not unkindly, but I feel my cheeks go red. She must see that I don't know how to respond, because she goes on. 'So, when you're in a dressage test, and you have to make a walk transition, how does your pony know he has to think about it? I mean, can he do what he just did in a test?'

Stupid woman, I think. I knew I shouldn't have come here, knew it was all a mistake. Now I'm going to spend the next hour being made to feel terrible. 'No.'

Rose nods. 'So, why don't you do that again, and then we'll talk about the rest. Hey, don't beat yourself up about it. You're far from being the only one. Everyone does it. Learn to ride every transition and you'll stop even thinking about it. Try it again, keeping a good trot until you're in walk.'

It's amazing how much we do - or don't - without being conscious of it. I push Jupiter back into a trot, and this time, I focus on keeping him correct right until I feel him fall to a walk. It's not even that hard.

'There you go, perfect!' Rose beams. 'You can let him have a breather a sec while we talk. So, how did the trot feel to you when you were going around before?'

If she'd have asked me a moment ago, I would have said good, but now I'm not sure. Instead I say what I know is true. 'He was forward and bending to the inside.'

She nods. 'That he was. Were you able to keep him straight and control him with your outside rein? How did his back feel?'

'He's not easy to sit on,' I tell her, which gets me out of answering the first question. 'I always feel like I'm going to bounce off his back.'

Rose moves on to another topic. 'Do you always work him quickly like that?' She doesn't say it meanly, but I still feel like my answer is going to be the wrong one.

'Eva, who I ride with, likes them to go with speed so they can find their own balance,' I say.

'You'll never find two people in the horse world with the same way of doing things,' Rose begins, 'but I tend to think that a horse can't possibly add on speed until he's balanced. Not on the flat, anyway. You need impulsion, but that's a completely different thing from speed. Think of a horse as having three parts - front, back, end. Now, we want him to use all three together. To get impulsion from behind, move through his back, right to the mouth, where you capture it. Does that make sense?' I nod. 'Now, to me on the ground, your pony's front and hind ends are working separately from each other, and you are stuck in the middle. The speed you're building up is escaping out the front end, and his hind end is just trying to keep up, and his back isn't getting a chance to do anything. And by going that quickly, you're running him off his balance.' She frowns. 'Does that make sense?'

I nod again, and this time I'm not fighting back tears. Yes, every word of that made perfect sense, and I just want to know more. Eva calls out orders all the time, but she never explains why.

'Can you pass me your whip?' Rose asks. I hand it to her, unsure what exactly is going through her head, and she takes a step back. 'Imagine this is your horse,' she says, holding the whip up, a hand at each end so that it's straight between her palms. 'What we want is for him to do *this.*' She draws her hands together, and the whip curves upwards, in a perfect arch. 'Not one bit of it is separate from the rest,' Rose explains. 'The whole thing curves together. Do you understand?'

'Yes,' I say, imagining that arch on a pony, imagining Jupiter curving like that from the his tail to the tip of his nose.

'Okay, then.' Rose smiles and hands me back the whip. 'Let's try again.'

chapter 2

I sit up tall, fighting the burning sensation in my limbs, and look straight ahead. Every muscle in my body is screaming for me to stop, for me to drop back to a walk and breathe, but I need to get a good transition. Jupiter flickers an ear, and I exhale, keeping my weight in my heels, and close my fingers on the outside rein, never letting go of the trot, holding the pony in a round frame even when he takes his first step of walk.

'Perfect,' Rose says. 'Now let your reins out and take a minute.'

She doesn't have to tell me twice. I give Jupiter his head, and he stretches his nose to the ground. I know how he feels.

And we haven't even started jumping yet.

Thirty minutes? I look away from my watch as quickly as I looked, not wanting Rose to think I'm fed up. Have we really only been going thirty minutes? There's even a triangle of sweat on Jupiter's neck - he never sweats, not unless he's just gone cross country. Certainly not after half an hour of flatwork.

'How many days a week does he work?' Rose asks.

'He works every weekend,' I say.

She nods. 'And?'

'Um, he works in the evening after school sometimes if I have time.'

'And when he's competing?' Rose is looking at Jupiter, not me, so I can't search her eyes for more information, for a clue.

I go for honesty. 'I don't understand...'

She looks at me now. 'How many days a week does he work during the event season? How many fitness days does he do?'

Haven't I just answered this? And what's a fitness day? 'He works weekends and maybe one other evening in the week.'

'So he gets ridden on Saturday, evented on Sunday, does nothing all week, and repeat?'

It sounds so bad when she says it like that. And she doesn't even know that unless I'm having a lesson, he rarely gets worked for more than half an hour due to the school being booked. 'Yeah.'

Rose presses her lips together and crosses her arms, tilting her head to the side, taking Jupiter in the way one does a painting. 'He's very stiff,' she begins, redirecting her gaze back towards me. 'Because he hasn't been working through his back, the muscles have seized, and it's his hind end that's compensating. It's deceptive because he's chunky, but he's quite weak behind. This isn't your fault,' she says quickly, 'but a horse that is ridden twice a week is not fit enough to compete, simple as that. You might get away with it for a while, but at some point it'll catch up with you, and the consequences will surface in the form of an injury.'

'Okay,' I say, not sure what else to say.

'To give you an idea,' Rose goes on, 'an event horse should be ridden six days out of seven - five at the very least - and if one of those days is the competition, that leaves you with five training days. Now what do we need to fit into those five days to get a horse event-ready?'

'Hacking?'

Rose starts counting on her fingers. 'Yep. So you can have a light hack on Tuesday, after a day off, and then maybe a small jump the next day, and then do canter sets on Thursday, hack again on Friday, and flatwork the day before the event. Does that sound right?'

I nod. 'It makes sense. But only one flatwork session?'

'They can school while they're hacking,' Rose says reasonably. 'Sometimes, depending how fit they are, they don't even need to see a school between events. And you wouldn't necessary stick to that every week, but you get the idea. A person who jogs once a week isn't fit to run a marathon, and a horse is no different. And the fitter your horse is, the lower the risk of sustaining injury.'

A strand of Jupiter's thick mane has fallen to the left, and I push it back to the correct side. 'I didn't know.'

'How can you? If you've never been taught. No one can be expected to just know these things.' The certainty with which she says the words decreases the guilt and shame I'm feeling. 'You don't know any better, and why should you?'

I keep my eyes on the grey mane that needs pulling. My fingers are still scarred from the last time I did so. 'He felt good in that last trot,' I say.

Rose nods encouragingly. 'He *was* good. That's what you need to work on. Balance and impulsion, not speed and inside flexion.'

'I will,' I say, taking my feet out the stirrups, ready to get off.

'Good. Hey, where're you going?'

I haven't swung off yet, and Rose's words make me sit back in the saddle. 'I thought we were...'

'You haven't cantered or jumped yet.' She pauses. 'Didn't you want to jump?'

'Yes. I mean, I *thought* I was, but then after that, I thought we were doing flatwork...' My voice drifts.

'We were warming up. You need a horse going well on the flat to jump, too. Okay, why don't you give him a loose canter on each rein, and then come back to trot and we'll do some pole work.'

'Okay.' Half an hour ago, I'd have pushed Jupiter straight into a canter, but now I focus on collecting the walk, getting into a nice trot, and then asking for a strike-off once he's round and moving with impulsion, Rose watching at the same time as she sets fences. His head comes up in the transition, but I ride it out, getting the best out of it I can.

'Well corrected,' Rose says.

Under Rose's watchful eye, I work Jupiter in trot again, repeating the same exercises I did earlier, though this time the results come much faster. He softens more quickly, relieving my arms of the usual rigid pressure while still staying on a contact, and soon I'm being called to go over a line of poles.

'He doesn't like trot poles,' I tell Rose worriedly. 'He often tries to canter and bounce them or take on all three as a jump. He's not good at jumping from trot full stop.'

Her eyes dart to the coloured poles, as though taking

them in for the first time, and then back to me. 'Oh. What a pity.'

The comment takes me so off guard that I laugh, fear gone.

Rose grins, too. 'I have yet to meet a horse that enjoys trot poles, but it has to be done. If you can't get over poles on the ground safely, then you sure shouldn't be raising them.'

I can't argue with that logic, and I turn Jupiter to the line, keeping the same trot I've been working for this whole session. As I knew he would, the pony snatches at the bit when he sees the poles, dressage forgotten, and I manage to keep him in trot over the first when he breaks into a canter, bouncing the next two as jumps and skidding across them in a horrible clatter.

'Okay.' Rose walks to the poles and rolls them back into place with the tip of her boot. 'What could've you done there?'

'I can't stop him once he decides to take off like that,' I say, feeling anxious again.

'But you knew he was going to take off?'

I nod. 'I can feel it from the turn.'

'Then why keep going and let him get away with it? At a competition, obviously you have to get over a fence no matter what, but we're not at a competition. If you feel he's going to take off with you, then turn him away. So long as you haven't presented him to the fence yet. But when it's through the turn like that, then keep turning. Keep circling him until he settles, so he doesn't know whether or not you're going to ask him to go over the poles and he stops anticipating. He can't drag you in like that.'

Feeling like I don't know a thing about riding, I get

Jupiter back into a trot, working him until he softens. As soon as I direct him to the poles, right through the turn, he grabs hold of the bit and rushes as if to take off, any attempts to check him met with dead pulling, and I keep turning right, bypassing the poles, and he's so surprised that he slows right down. Rose praises the effort and I keep going, another attempt. Jup doesn't rush through the turn this time, and I think I'm going to be okay, but then, just one stride from the poles, he surges forward, and in a panic, I pull, confusing him, and we hit the first before veering off to the left.

'So, you know what's wrong with that,' Rose says.

'I stopped him too late?'

She nods. 'If you're going to turn away from an obstacle, you have to make it clear. You can't have him wondering if he's going to jump at the last minute because that'll just teach him to stop. No matter what you have in the last three strides, you have to go with it. Keep going, try again.'

I don't know what it is - the better trot, the repetition, just knowing that there's no way I'll be allowed to leave this sand school until getting the exercise right - but we *do* manage in the end. Jupiter trots over the poles, unhappily at first, until we're going through the line without worries, and the way his back lifts through the air is something I've never felt before, not even jumping.

'There you go, what's wrong with that?' Rose beams. 'Just so you don't think I'm mad, I'll actually get some of these poles off the ground for you.'

Two poles are made into a cross, with the third left in front, Rose pacing the distance between them. I'm not even going to bother mentioning how much Jupiter despises placing poles, because I know what her answer will be. *What a pity.* He hates trot jumping, too, but I might as well just get this over with, and if it goes wrong then it's not like I'm to blame.

Jupiter floats to the fence, his rhythm remaining steady, and I wonder if he's even seen it, even noticed the pole on the ground in front of the cross, but I don't have time to think, because he moves over it, and effortlessly canters one stride to the fence. It's a small cross rail, a warm-up jump, nothing more, but the second I spend in the air, the swinging of Jupiter's body, the softness in his back, the general feeling of togetherness, is different from anything I'm used to.

Rose holds her hands out to the side, smiling at me. 'Now what was wrong with that?' she mocks. 'Beautiful. Absolutely spot on. I know it's not very high, but there's no reason it should be any different over bigger fences. Once you have the rhythm nailed, height is easy. How did it feel to you?'

'It felt amazing,' I say. 'He was so... *comfortable.* And he didn't try to rush out all.'

I'm so happy. I *should* be happy. But what's weird is how happy Rose is. She's just as - if not more - excited to help someone have a breakthrough as the person in question is themselves. 'No, he didn't. It was perfect. Do it again?'

Ten minutes later, clearing a jump that is far from being the biggest I've ever gone over but definitely feels the nicest, I can't wipe the grin off my face. I let my reins out when I come back to walk, showering Jupi's neck with praise. Rose walks up to him and does the same.

'You should be really proud of yourself,' she tells me. 'I know I was pushing you a bit but you pushed through it and did amazingly. Well done.'

'Thank you.'

'Well, that looked fantastic!' She's been so quiet this whole lesson, sitting unnoticed at the side of the ring, that I'd forgotten Mum was even here. 'I've never seen you two look so good. Thank you so much, Rose.'

She shrugs off the praise. 'I didn't do anything, it was all Sybil. And he's a cracking little pony. Just-' Rose breaks off, considering her words, and goes on. 'I don't want to step on anyone's toes, and I know this might be hard in your situation, but if you could just up the fitness. Keep working him as you did today and you should be absolutely fine, but he *is* stiff in the back and weak behind, and I really think he could benefit from going out more. Hacking's obviously the best, but whatever you can do...'

Mum nods. 'Absolutely. Sybil's eventing next weekend, anyway.'

'I'll try to work him as you said,' I chime in. 'I'll see if there's anyone to go for a hack with.'

'And we'll discuss things together later,' Mum goes on, her blue eyes meeting mine, 'but I certainly know that *I* would love her to come here and train with you.'

'Don't worry,' Rose says, shaking her head. 'Take a little time to think and discuss it over. You've got your event coming up, anyway, so just focus on that for now, and see what happens after.'

For all my reservations about coming here, I suddenly wish we could just makes arrangements, set it in stone, but then I remember Eva, and how I don't want to let her down, either. But in the two years I've been keeping Jupiter with her, she's never given me as much time and thought as Rose has today.

'Brace yourselves,' Rose says as we all walk across the courtyard, me leading Jupiter and undoing his noseband at the same time, as a car pulls up beside the white farmhouse - presumably Rose's home - opposite. 'Our old dog passed away last month,' she explains, 'and Ben just took the kids to pick up the new puppy this afternoon. Consider yourselves warned.'

Car doors fly open, voices shriek, and then two almost identical figures are running towards us, girls who look like mini versions of Rose, with two just-as-identical puppies, lead ropes attached to their collars.

'What is this?' Rose says, looking down at the black and white blurs that are rushing all around us. Jupiter has always liked dogs, but even he plants his feet and snorts, which doesn't escape Rose's attention. 'Not around the horses,' she snaps quickly, the firmest I've heard her sound. 'You know better.' She pauses as the young girls get their respective puppies under control. 'Hey, that's my best lead rope. Why are there two of them?'

'Daddy said it was all right,' one of them sings, her voice both loud and confident enough to make me think she must be Mackenzie - the chatty one.

'We only chose one when we went to see them,' Rose says, her eyes meeting those of her husband as he crosses the courtyard. He's tall and blond, and although he's athletic and dressed for the country, I immediately think that he doesn't come across as a rider.

He shrugs, looking at his daughters. 'What can I say, they're stubborn like their mother.' He looks up again and smiles at us, holding a hand out to Mum. 'Nice to meet you.'

'This is Ben,' Rose says. 'Ben, meet Maya and Sybil. And you're not actually going to believe it, but Maya and I were at Pony Club together.'

'Ah, the horse world,' Ben says, shaking my hand too, and then even greeting Jupiter with a scratch on the forehead. 'Because the rest of the world isn't small enough.'

Mum laughs. 'Exactly.'

Farther along from us, the puppies catch sight of a pigeon, and they break into a run, dragging their handlers across the concrete. Mackenzie and Jemima shriek, and Rose sighs loudly.

'If you fall over again, Jem, I'm not looking after you,' she calls. And then to us, 'Don't get too used to Ben, he's about to be banished, because the *only* instruction he had to follow today was to only bring one dog home.'

'On that note, I'll be off.' He smiles politely at us again, but there's warmth to it. 'Kenzie, Mima, take the puppies inside or Mummy's sending them back,' he calls, which is enough to make the girls hurry.

As they all disappear from earshot, Rose shakes her head and pulls a face at us. 'I knew that would happen. The only reason I didn't go myself was because I knew we'd end up coming home with *three*. Don't tell Ben I said that,' she adds. 'Oh, let me get you some water,' she goes on as I reach the trailer, looking at Jupiter, and before I can offer to do so myself, Rose is off, heading to the wash bay. Mum makes the most of the opportunity to seek out my gaze, her expression midway between "I told you so" and "Pretty pretty please". I look away, not wanting to get into any conversation now, and focus on Jupiter's saddle, running the stirrups up and undoing the girth. He's drenched beneath the saddle cloth, grey coat black.

'Look at that,' Mum says, sounding impressed as she steps up to Jupi and touches her hand to his back. 'He never usually sweats, does he? And he didn't even do that much.'

Jupiter's bridle is off and he stands tied to the trailer when Rose comes back carrying two buckets of water, one half full with a sponge in it, the other full to the brim, which she puts down in front of him. 'There you go,' she says, scratching Jup's neck affectionately as he lowers his nose to drink. I kneel beside him to remove his tendon boots.

'I was just telling Sybil that I've never seen him sweat like that before,' Mum tells Rose. 'The only time you can get him to sweat is if he's going XC. Amazing!'

Jupiter stops drinking to look up at us, water dripping from his lips, as though he doesn't think his perspiration is quite so *amazing*.

'You can work incorrectly for three hours without breaking a sweat, and you can exhaust yourself in a few minutes if you do it right,' Rose says. 'And really, if they're working correctly, they shouldn't need to do much more than forty-five minutes. Not in a school. It might not have looked like much, but this will have been hard for him.'

Tell me about it, I think as I start rolling up bandages, my own muscles and limbs in agony.

'So,' Mum goes on, 'I know Sybil and I need to have a little discussion' - she says it the way one would talk about fairies in front of a child, so obviously just humouring them - 'but if she *were* to come here with Jupiter, that would be okay? We only discussed it a little the other day, but you have space and whatnot? And you offer DIY?'

Rose nods. 'Yes to all three. I have two stables empty, though I have a schooling livery arriving in one soon, but I'm sure there's no rush for the other. Standard DIY is fine, but I'm pretty flexible with liveries, so you can vary it any which way. I have a girl who helps me, Leah, and you can ask us for anything. And if you wanted to avoid having to source your own bedding and feed et cetera, what I do a lot is allow you to just get it straight from me and I add it on, if you want to save yourself the hassle. But if you want to do standard DIY and take care of everything yourself then that's no problem.'

'No, no,' Mum says, 'I like what you said.' She looks at me. 'The number of times we've had to go hunting for a bag of shavings because the local supplier was out.'

'Mine are on straw, though.'

'Doesn't straw make them colic?' I say, picking up the next bandage. The fact that Mum is going ahead and making arrangements without my consent is getting on my nerves.

Mum looks at Rose, silently either apologising for my rudeness or finding it humorous - I can't tell - and Rose smiles. 'Everyone has their own opinion. Colic is most commonly caused by a lack of roughage, which is why some people think it's safer to stable them on straw because should they run out of hay, they can pick a few mouthfuls of straw and have something in their system. I for one never leave my horses without hay, and don't ever see them eat the straw, and I've' - she breaks off to jog to the nearest building, a hay barn, and knocks her hand on the wooden door - 'as of yet never had a horse colic in all the years I've been doing this.'

My eyes go wide. 'Never?' At Eva's, where horses are stabled on shavings and their hay is rationed, as she also advises the few DIYs to do, too, colic is a relatively common occurrence.

'Never. I've always given them bran and sugar beet in their feeds, too, which keeps their systems moving and prevents blockages. So, I use straw. And I also think a straw bed is a lot nicer for them than shavings. I did have some horses on shavings once, and all of them got bad frogs because it dried their feet out in summer, and didn't keep them dry at all in winter.'

'Good old straw beds are all we used to have,' Mum says. The way she says it, you'd think she'd ridden Advanced herself and not just had a scruffy pony.

'I understand some horses need to be stabled on shavings or paper, particularly those with allergies,' Rose says, 'but I like straw, and mine are all fine on it.'

'As Jupiter would be,' Mum adds determinedly. 'And do you turn out?'

'Of course. Every day without fail. All day if weather permits. Does he go out with others?'

Mum answers before I can. 'He barely goes out at all! There are only a few fields between all the horses, and they're not even allowed out if the weather's bad so as not to churn up the ground.'

'He used to be with others,' I say. 'Before I got him.'

'Okay. Well, whatever you're comfortable with. I only asked because my daughters' ponies are out together, and they stay out all night in summer, too, so I thought maybe you'd like to turn him out with them.'

'That would be lovely! Wouldn't that be lovely, Sybil?'

What would be lovely is no mucking out, but I don't say that. 'Maybe,' I agree.

'And what about lessons?' Mum asks. She snaps her fingers. 'Which reminds me, I need to know how much I owe you for today.'

Rose shakes her head. 'Nope, first one's free.' Mum starts to protest, but she goes on. 'Think of it as a trial, I do it for everyone. Lesson prices are on the piece of paper I gave you the other day, but obviously if Sybil were riding in the school while I'm around and just needed a few pointers I wouldn't charge for that.' Rose laughs. 'I'm not exactly a businesswoman. But I'm able to be like that because Ben's job allows him to run the house while I just keep this place ticking.'

'The school's often free?' I ask, wanting to confirm what Rose said earlier.

'Yes, most of the time. I ride mine in the morning, and even if I'm in there that doesn't stop you from coming in. It's only if I'm teaching a lesson, really. But you can ride on the grass beyond the paddocks, where there are a few cross country jumps, and the hacking's good here. You have to go on the lanes a little to connect to bridle paths, but because everyone in Newmarket knows to slow down for horses, it's pretty safe.'

'I think it's all wonderful,' Mum says, looking around as though she were seeing it for the first time. 'I don't want to hold you up much longer, but thank you so much for your time today and being so helpful. I think I know what we're going to do, but I'll get back to you as soon as possible'

'Oh, no worries. Take your time, focus on the event this week and you can get back to me the next. No rush, it's a big decision. Thank you for coming. Good luck at your event next weekend,' she says to me.

'Thank you.'

'Well,' Mum says as we're pulling out of the yard, both hands on the steering wheel, 'I think this is kind of a no-brainer, don't you?'

I cross my arms, staring resolutely out of the window. The wooden stables, the uneven courtyard, the happy horses. 'Maybe.'

chapter 3

Jupiter flies over the log, landing far out, and although I wouldn't have thought anything of the jump a week ago, today it doesn't feel right.

'Just jump the palisade on an angle once before going to the start,' Eva says to me when I pass her near the entrance to the cross country warm-up, where she is standing by the whiteboard the steward has written riders' numbers on. I'm next.

I bring Jupiter back to a walk, glancing at the start box in time to see a heavy skewbald set off towards the first fence. Jupiter stretches his neck out, and I notice how his sides are heaving, nostrils flared. 'Are you sure he's all right?' I ask.

Eva's eyes snap to mine. She's the same age as Rose, and yet she manages to look both younger and older at the same time. Younger because there's this air of inexperience to her, which has been particularly noticeable this past week, like somebody trying to pass themselves off as more than they are. And older because she's strict, possesses a conviction that she is always right, and is almost incapable of having a laugh. 'What are you talking about? Of course he's fine.' She looks across the warm-up ring, at another rider from the yard, and calls out an instruction.

But I go on. 'It's just that he didn't feel quite right.' That's an understatement. Ever since the lesson with Rose, nothing has felt right. When I got Jupiter back to Eva's that evening, when I lowered the ramp and led him out of the trailer, I just felt sad. The immaculate yard seemed cold, the people distant, and suddenly I wished I were anywhere else. That evening I planned to ride every day the next week, to work on what Rose talked about, but nothing went to plan. The school was always booked, nobody wanted to go hacking with me and my attempt to do so alone was a terrifying half hour of spooking and dodging traffic. When I did get time in the saddle, the exercises I did with Rose weren't working, the results not the same, and when Eva spotted me in the school, failing miserably, she shouted that everything I was doing was wrong and gave me different instructions. It was ridiculous really, that I was questioning my coach's methods after just one lesson with somebody else, who could have just as easily been wrong, but the thing was, I knew she wasn't. What I felt, how well Jupiter went, was all the proof I needed. Horses don't lie.

The dressage this morning was a usual disappointment. We executed the movements, but Jupiter was fighting me the whole time, carrying his head high, and it just felt awkward. When I started warming him up for show jumping, it was like being in a car with a flat engine. I don't know if he's always been like this and I'm only just noticing, but there was just nothing in the tank. I desperately tried to think back to past warm-ups, tried to remember if he was always this way and I didn't know any better because I'd never experienced the feeling of connection I did in last week's lesson. There was no roundness to his neck, no softness to his back, no feeling of security. But then Eva came into the middle of the ring, setting fences and calling me to the jumps, and I pushed the thoughts aside. Not a single jump felt as nice as the ones at Rose's did, and for one of the first times in my life, I would have given anything not to be riding. In the ring, when the start bell sounded, Jupiter perked up, excitement at the prospect of jumping a course overriding any fatigue he was feeling, and although he jumped clear, he also jumped the whole course by braille, which isn't like him. Show jumping is his reliable phase, because he hates to touch a fence, which made me suspicious, but when we came out of the ring, Eva told me that rattling the poles was entirely my fault, that I rode without impulsion and buried him into every fence, so I didn't know what to think.

But now I'm sure he's tired. 'He feels tired,' I tell Eva, to which she responds by pulling a condescending face. 'He hasn't given with his back,' I go on. 'He feels completely rigid…' I shake my head. 'I don't think he's right.'

'Don't be ridiculous,' Eva snaps. 'He's absolutely fine.'

'Three-seven-five,' the steward says to me. 'You're up.'

Eva's eyes dart to the horseless start box, where another steward is waiting. 'You haven't got time to jump again now, so go on. He's fine, get over it.'

My nerves are frazzled as I trot Jupiter to the start box, passing Mum who is holding on to both dogs, and the steward tells me I have thirty seconds. Jupiter flickers an ear towards me as we start trotting around the start, and my own ears start ringing. Nothing feels right. This is all wrong.

I don't want to be here.

'Our next starter will be number 375 Sybil Dawson, riding Mrs Johanna Atkinson's Ardmore Galaxy. They show jumped clear to remain on their dressage score of 42.6.'

'Ten seconds.'

'Get him moving as soon as you're out the start box,' Eva calls behind me. 'Wake him up, give him a reminder at the first fence.'

'Five, four, three, two, one, GO! Good luck.' I don't really hear the last two words, a distant sound, but they're always there. The start box countdown never changes, and Jupiter knows it as well as I do, lurching into a gallop at the word go. I stand in my stirrups, hands up his neck, pushing away every bad thought I've had today. Once you're on course, everything else fades away. There's no place for uncertainty.

The first fence is an inviting roll top, and Jupiter sees his own stride and clears it easily. I set aside my earlier reservations even more resolutely, because clearly he's fine. Eva knows far more than I do, so I've obviously just got it into my head that something's wrong and convinced myself of it even though it's not true.

The course isn't any more challenging than others we've been around, but BE90 isn't tiny either, especially not for a fourteen-two pony. But Jupiter loves cross country, and he's game for everything. He starts off strong, as he always does, keen to jump. With every fence the pressure in my arms diminishes, until there's almost no weight. When we pass the halfway mark, Jupiter isn't pulling at all, and I smile to myself. Maybe I have been doing okay since the lesson with Rose, if I've already managed to stop my pony yanking my arms out.

The next fence is a trakehner, and I click my tongue as I start turning Jupiter towards it, preparing him. But he barely reacts, and his head is low when we come to the fence. I kick, for want of another idea, and we scramble over the jump, but I hear Jupiter's feet touch the log, and I hit the saddle hard on landing.

'Go on,' I yell, finding my two-point position again to urge Jupiter on. He doesn't accelerate, just drops his head lower, and I can hear his every breath. But that's normal, isn't it? I can hear horses breathe on TV when I watch Badminton, and they're not exactly lacking fitness. Besides, all horses get tired towards the end of a course.

A combination is next, and I manage to get Jupiter together in time for the first, and we hit the two strides easily. Of course we do, he's fine. Just a bit tired, which is normal. And we've only got a few fences to go.

In the galloping stretch to the next fence, Jupiter seems to lose even more energy, which I wouldn't have thought possible on a cross country course. He's dropping onto the forehand, still blowing hard, and I feel like I can barely keep him in canter. I gather him up the best I can for the corner, trying to move him on, but I know we're going to have to jump it on a short stride.

I sit up for the fence, squeezing my legs against Jupiter's sides. His ears swivel forward, locking on to the jump, and I click my tongue for encouragement. I lean forward on take-off stride, relieved we've agreed on the same one, but something's not right. Like Jupiter tries to push off his back legs and can't. No power, no petrol in the tank. But Jupiter doesn't refuse, and he still goes, still tries to jump. We hit the fence, loud enough that I close my eyes with a sense of foreboding, and for a moment I think we're going to land safely, but Jupiter falls to his knees, and before I know it the ground is rushing towards me, and I fall to the side, rolling out of the way. I jump up as soon as my feet find the dirt, relieved to see Jupiter getting up too, and I hurry to his side. He looks dazed, not understanding what just happened. It's probably the first time he's fallen in his life. But I'm more concerned by how much he's blowing, how his nostrils flare and his sides heave. The fence steward is coming up beside me, but I'm already in control, undoing Jupiter's flash noseband and loosening the girth.

'You okay? Get him walking,' the steward says with concern, and she doesn't have to tell me twice.

'Come on, boy,' I say, clicking my tongue as I pull on Jupiter's reins. Any feeling of disappointment at being eliminated is overridden by concern for him. I'm shaking, be it caused by fear or colliding with the ground I don't know.

Jupiter steps forward, albeit stiffly, and I run the stirrups up as he walks, muttering words of reassurance. 'I'm sorry,' I tell him. 'I knew you weren't right. I'm sorry. It'll never happen again, I promise you. It'll never happen again.'

'He seems happy,' Rose says, walking up beside me.

Happy is an understatement for how Jupiter looks right now. He's been at Rose's one hour, in the field for half, and he's made himself right at home. After letting him calm down in his new stable for a little while, Rose suggested turning him out, on his own for now, giving him the day to settle. Jupiter came out of the stable eagerly, as though he were competition-ready, but as soon as I led him to the paddock and unclipped his rope, he put his head down to eat, then rolled, then starting grazing again, and he hasn't moved since. There are other horses in the paddocks around him, but he isn't interested in them. And even though he isn't moving much, there's a brightness to his eye that I haven't seen in a long time.

'He loves it,' I tell Rose, throwing the rope down by the gate post. I kept it in hand in case he decided to start galloping and being stupid and injure himself, should I have to hurry to catch him, but it's clear that won't be the case.

This past week has been the toughest of my life, which is saying something because a few months ago the life I had was shredded to pieces. The vet came out the Monday after the event, by when Jupiter was walking normally, and performed a clinical test which brought few answers, which I guess is a good thing. I was sure there was nothing medically wrong with Jupiter, but the vet performed flexions and made me trot the gelding up and stick him on the lunge, all of which was fine. Probably a freak fall, she said, and all stiffness would go away. And he'd possibly suffered a mild case of azoturia. But Eva had a different idea. She was adamant there was a problem with Jupiter's stifle, that that was why he couldn't push off his back legs, and that the joint should be injected in case and Jupiter put on box rest. The thought of big needles being stuck into my horse's joints made me squirm. And after the weekend I was even more convinced that Jupiter's problems came from not moving *enough,* so restricting all movement was the last thing I wanted to do. Rose had told me that he wasn't fit, had said he was weak behind, and that was exactly what I felt on that course. Jupiter was tired, and not strong enough to make up for it, and yet he still tried to jump. Heart of gold, as always. Wasn't worked properly and wasn't worked enough. Meanwhile Eva went on talking about testing this joint and that joint and the thought of my pony being kept inside indefinitely, and having needles stuck in his limbs made me sick. That evening, after speaking to the vet, I called Rose. I spoke for a while, though most of it was frantic babble, and to her credit she set my mind at rest.

'I'll tell you what I'd do if he were mine,' she said. 'He hasn't been working correctly, we both know that, and before interfering, I think he just needs to get fit. Rehab him this summer, start from scratch, get him walking, let him spend some time out, moving around, just being a horse, and take it from there. Then we'll see what we're dealing with. If he's still not right after that, you can start looking deeper for an underlying problem. But most injuries are caused by how a horse is worked. People always want a diagnosis and a quick fix, when really that's not how things go. But that's only what I would do, it doesn't mean it's what's right.'

'So, just get him fit?' I said.

'That's my opinion. Fitness is everything. Get muscles in the right place, get his body strong, get his lungs strong, and you'd be amazed. If ever something like this happened again, then you can look deeper for a problem, but then it's tricky once you get into that because no horse is perfect and most of them go their whole lives with issues beneath the surface. I don't think there's anything wrong with Jupiter, though. He just needs to be worked right, fed right, able to be a horse. I think all he needs is three months of fitness work, but that's just my opinion.'

'That's what I want to do.' Mum was standing across from me in our boxed-up kitchen, face tear-stained from the past days' trauma, and she nodded encouragingly at me. She'd barely said a word when I asked her for Rose's number. 'I want to do what you said. That's what I want to do.'

That was two weeks ago now. We drove the last of our belongings to the cottage down the road yesterday, then Mum and I set off early this morning to collect Jupiter from Eva's. I'd been walking him every day since the event, and turning out whenever possible. When the school was booked, which was most of the time, I'd simply walk him up and down the barn aisle, ignoring other boarders' looks of irritation. Leading him off the trailer this morning, arriving in the inviting yard, I felt relieved.

'Do you think he's okay to leave?' I ask Rose. Now that I'm here, now that I know Rose, I can't imagine there was ever a time I didn't have her to rely on.

'I think he's fine,' Rose says, nodding, 'but you know him better than I do. If you want to go home for a bit, someone can keep an eye on him and bring him in or call you if something goes wrong. I'll be here the rest of the day, but I just have to go pick a horse up in a minute, but I should be back within an hour.'

'Okay.' I start walking with Rose, back towards the stables. 'So... what's the horse you're picking up like?' Eva's never chatty, at least not with younger students. If she so much as said a few words to me outside of a lesson, I would be buzzing with excitement at having been addressed. Rose doesn't seem like that, and I'd love it if she liked me enough to make conversation. Though I wasn't that nice to her the first time I was here, so I might have already blown that.

She smiles. 'Your guess is as good as mine,' she jokes. 'No, that's not true, I have seen her before. She's a fourteen-two Thoroughbred-type - crossed with Arab, I think - and she's eight. She belongs to some people I know, a well-to-do family not far away, hunting parents, and the kids event. So this pony was bought for the youngest daughter a few years ago, who, between you and me, isn't the best rider, and she wasn't the easiest ride anyway, but the girl did kind of muck her up. Pretty as anything, but sensitive, and she's just lost her way and when Beatrix moved off ponies they couldn't sell her.'

'Couldn't they sell her as a broodmare?' I ask.

Rose nods. 'Exactly right. That's what they did last year. They put her to a lovely warmblood pony stallion and decided to keep her to breed. She foaled in March, and kicked the poor thing to death within minutes.'

I gape at her. 'No?'

'Yep. Anxious mares like that can go either way - they're either the best or worst mothers. So that was a few months ago, and one of their grooms has started bringing her back into work, but they don't really have the time or knowledge to deal with it, so they've asked if I can school her enough to sell her this summer. They're nice people, really, because most would probably send her to the kennels and be done with it. And they don't want to just give her away, because once you give a horse away for nothing you know not only are they not going to go somewhere good, but they're just going to keep being passed around. I know the family from the eventing circuit, but I haven't seen the pony in years so I don't really know what she's going to be like. I remember liking her back then, though.'

'Yeah?'

'Oh, she was lovely. Nuts, yes, but she could jump. I don't really see how I'll get her foolproof enough to sell in a couple of months, though, but we'll see.'

After Rose drives off, assuring me that Leah will keep

an eye on Jupiter, I walk home to do some unpacking for a while. The house is set back from the country lane, and for the first time, walking to it from the yard, the thought of it being home excites me. It's one of two semi-detached cottages, a small fence running along the front garden as a barrier, and the dwellings are like mirror images. Small and narrow, two storeys of red bricks, gable roofs. Next to the wooden front door is a diamond window, the tiny panes of glass as old as the house itself. There's another garden out back, too, which backs on to some farm land around which a footpath runs - perfect for walking the dogs.

The windows are open as I approach the cottage, and the front door swings ajar before I even reach it.

'Sybil,' Mum says, her smile wide. I don't know whether she's truly ecstatic or if the enthusiasm is purely for my and Gabe's sake, but she's been like this since we moved here last night. 'How's our favourite pony?'

'You'd think he's been there all his life,' I tell her.

Mum smiles even wider. 'That's so great. I'm so happy. Do you not need to watch him?'

I shake my head. 'Rose has asked Leah to keep an eye on him, but she thinks he's fine. I'll go back in a bit, but Rose has just gone to pick a horse up. She said she should be back by twelve.'

'Why don't you go walk the dogs with Gabe? That way I can stay here and keep unpacking. He's getting the leads on them.' She looks over her shoulder, mumbles something to my brother that I can't hear, and then steps out, followed by two lumps of dog. They last saw me two hours ago, but the dogs run up to me as though I were returning from a year-long trip, dragging Gabe with them, and I drop to my knees to return the affection.

'Down, Frodo,' I say to the rambunctious Labrador Retriever, pushing him to the side to reach the more timid dog. 'Come here, El,' I say softly, and the pit bull approaches me, leaning her body against mine for attention.

'Which one do you want?' Gabe asks, holding the leads out to me. There are only a few years between us, but Gabe is half my size, both shorter and skinnier, all angles. The thick glasses he wears accentuate his awkwardness, and he speaks with a lisp I no longer notice unless somebody is rude enough to point it out.

I shrug. 'You pick.'

He passes me Eleven's lead, which I happily take. El spent two years at the pound, after being abandoned by her owners, and nobody would re-home her because of her breed. We'd already experienced one rescue dog in Frodo, whose time spent homeless was nothing compared to El, and were looking at some other dogs at the pound last November when Gabe and I spotted the pit bull sitting in a corner of her cage, against the back wall, staring at the ground. For all of her nerves, Eleven - as we later named her after a character in our favourite TV series - came straight up to us when we addressed her, wagging her tail, looking so hopeful that none of us could bear to leave her. She has remained just as sweet to this day.

'Hey, look,' Gabe says to Mum and me quietly, looking to the side. 'There's our neighbour.'

The cottage adjacent to ours is occupied by a retired widower who doesn't seem to be one for talking, but our other closest neighbour, the detached house farther along, has been a mystery up to now. Both cottages could fit inside the building and leave room to spare. The house is square, also red brick, and almost looks grand, but it's overshadowed by a feeling of being haunted. The front door is dark, the windows gothic, and the garden around it is not only flowerless but overgrown. In the times we've been here, we've never seen anyone enter or leave the house - until now. A guy, possibly a couple of years younger than Mum, has just stepped out of the front door, not dressed the way you'd expect someone who can afford such a house to be. His skin is pale, brown hair ruffled, he wears tracksuit bottoms and a plaid shirt, and a white cat walks at his heels. Frodo starts to growl, and I seize his collar and scold him before he has a chance to do any more. He's fine with cats really, just pretends he isn't.

'He looks pleasant,' Gabe says sarcastically.

'Shh,' Mum snaps. And then, 'Let's go say hello and introduce ourselves.'

'Or let's not,' I say.

'Don't be ridiculous. He's our neighbour, it's the polite thing to do.'

'The polite thing would be for *him* to introduce himself,' Gabe points out, but Mum has already started walking, and we follow.

'Hello there,' she calls, waving for effect. The guys stops walking halfway down his short drive and looks at us as though we were aliens. 'I'm sorry to disturb you, I just thought we should come introduce ourselves. I'm Maya, and these are my children Sybil and Gabe, and we've just moved into Bluebell Cottage. Say hello, kids,' she adds, frowning at our silence.

'Hello,' Gabe and I say robotically.

'Hello,' the guy says. It's just one word, but he speaks the sort of posh Queen's English you'd expect from someone who attended Eton.

'This is such a lovely area,' Mum goes on. 'Everything is so pretty. We're so excited to be living here. I know we're not settled in yet, but just know that should you ever need something in future, don't hesitate to knock on our door, be it a cup of sugar or a drive to A & E because you've broken a limb. Okay? I'm sorry, I didn't catch your name.'

Because he didn't say it, I think. Frodo strains himself against his lead, moving forward a step, and the guy's white cat hisses.

'Liam,' he finally says, eyes going from his cat to the dogs and back again.

'Liam,' Mum repeats, still smiling. 'Well, I should get back to unpacking and the kids to walking the dogs, but it was very nice to meet you, Liam.'

Liam nods slowly, turns on his heels, and starts walking back to the house, white cat following. It's only when the door is closed behind me that it strikes me. 'What did he come outside for? He literally stepped out, walked ten paces, and then went back inside again!'

'Maybe he's a vampire,' Gabe says. 'Or a werewolf, and he can't stay in daylight for too long.'

'You two need to stay away from fantasy and science fiction,' Mum says. 'He was perfectly nice, probably just shy. That doesn't give us any right to judge him. Now, take those dogs for a walk so Sybil can get back to the yard.'

Having my pony within walking distance is definitely something I could get used to. Head out the front door, walk a few hundred metres down the small country road, and I'm at the yard. It's almost like keeping him at home. And just a little farther on and I can get to Freya's, too. She said she'll come see Jupiter as soon as she can, but she and her mum are at Brand Hall today, watching Leo compete in the British Pony Championships. It's a three-hour drive, so they're only seeing the dressage and cross country, not returning tomorrow for the show jumping. Not that we'll be able to go for long rides together anytime soon even if she does get him.

Jupiter doesn't look like he's moved since I left him, standing in the far corner of the paddock, picking at what spring grass remains. He lifts his head when I cluck to him, looks at me standing at the fence, and resumes grazing.

'Ignore me, why don't you,' I mutter.

'Hello! Is that your pony? He's so cute! What's his name?'

The voice makes me jump, and I turn to see one of Rose's daughters, now addressing Jupiter and not me, leaning over the fence beside me. Must be the chatty one. Is that Mackenzie?

'That's my pony Jupiter,' I say. 'Well, he's not really mine, I loan him. I rode him here a few weeks ago, when you got your puppies.'

Mackenzie frowns. 'Uh, I don't remember. Have you seen our puppies? They're a mix of Springer Spaniel and Border Collie and Jack Russell. One's mine and one's Jemima's.'

I nod, suddenly dreading that this is what being in this yard is going to be like: constantly bugged by kids. 'Yep. You had them out last time.'

'Oh.' Mackenzie pauses. 'Have you seen Cinder?'

'I don't know who Cinder is.'

'You have to come see her, then,' she says, grabbing hold of my hand and dragging me towards the yard. 'She's in her stable because I just finished riding her. Mum's not here, which means I'm only allowed to ride if I don't jump or fall off, because she hasn't got time to look after me if I hurt myself.' I try not to laugh, but it doesn't escape Mackenzie's attention, though she misunderstands my amusement because she says, 'No, really, it's true.'

'I believe you,' I say. *Yes*, I think, that's definitely something Rose would say.

Mackenzie pulls me into a stable where a dark bay pony stands, picking at some hay. On the one hand, she's plainer than you'd expect the pony of a professional rider's daughter to be, but she's also gorgeous. Not flashy, dark bay without markings, nicely put together, and a kind eye.

'She's nice,' I say.

Mackenzie drapes herself across the mare, hanging from her neck, and the pony doesn't even blink. 'She's the best pony in the whole wide world.' Then in another breath, 'You can ride her if you want.'

The comment surprises me. Most kids consider their ponies too precious to be ridden by anyone other than their supposedly talented selves. 'Oh, that's okay.'

'I mean it,' Mackenzie says seriously, looking me in the eye. 'You can ride her if you want,' she repeats. 'Do you want to ride her now?'

'That's okay. Maybe another time,' I offer.

She shrugs. 'Okay. I'm going to put her in the field now.' And with that she's putting a head collar on at full speed and leading the mare out of the box with all the confidence of a kid who's been around horses her whole life.

The ponies are in the farthest paddock, and I can see Mackenzie at the gate in the distance when a lorry pulls into the yard. Rose is at the steering wheel, and as she slows the vehicle to pull up onto the concrete, the horse inside kicks.

'Sorry about that,' Rose says to me, climbing down from the cab. 'No one was around when I got there, and they'd left her in the barn alone while all the other horses were turned out and-' She breaks off, shaking her head. 'Anyway. Still loaded well after all that, bless her.' She undoes the bolts at the back of the lorry and jumps up to lower the ramp. 'Watch yourself, mind. I don't know her enough to know if she'll do anything stupid.'

'What is she like?' I ask, just as Leah comes over the help Rose with the ramp, and I feel silly for not offering to do so. Though Rose doesn't say anything about it.

'Um, thinner than I was expecting, to be honest,' she says. 'I wasn't expecting her to be fit, but I thought she'd have more weight on her. She's a fussy eater, apparently. Just what I need. It's bad enough getting them sale-ready in two months when you aren't trying to put weight on them. Oh well, we'll see what happens. Her shoes are loose, too, so I'm going to have to do that asap.' Rose slides through the partitions, and I can hear her murmur words of reassurance to the pony. 'Okay,' she calls to Leah. 'Everyone out the way?'

I hug the nearest wall and wait for the mare to come down the ramp. I'm expecting commotion, a spectacle of flying hooves and teeth, but she walks down even more calmly than Jupiter did.

Like Rose said, she's underweight. She's not critical, and certainly doesn't look like a rescue case, but that's partly because she's clearly been cared for. Her bay coat shines with dapples, mane pulled to the width of a hand, tail and feathers trimmed, un-bandaged black legs straight, limbs clean. Rose pats her on the shoulder and the mare turns her head, revealing a heart-shaped star on her elegant, dished face. She wears a leather head collar with a nameplate, but I can't read the letters from here. Rose pats the mare again, and steps back to let her take in her surroundings.

'What do you think?' she says to me.

'She's gorgeous,' I say. Pretty, elegant, athletic. If only *crazy* weren't added on to that list.

'Agreed. What I like is she's more like a little horse than a pony. Come on,' Rose tells the mare, clicking her tongue, and she leads her to the stables. She goes around the side of the main courtyard, to a box on the end of the building I haven't noticed before. The door is on the other side, but a window looks out towards the stables, so that there are other horses in sight. 'I'll leave her to settle for a bit,' she says when she's unclipped the rope and walked out of the box. The mare goes straight to the window, pushing her head through, and looks out at the few horses in the yard, letting out a small whinny. When she turns her head to the right I notice a speck of white in her left eye, on the edge of the iris, and I can make out the letters engraved on the nameplate of her leather head collar, reading the words aloud.

'Ace of Hearts.'

Rose chuckles. 'I know. Not very original, what with her marking, but it is a perfect heart, it has to be said.'

'Does she have a stable name?'

'Uh.' Rose winces. 'Kind of. They call her Maggot.'

'Maggot,' I repeat sceptically.

'Not a name they gave her intentionally, so they say. She earned that one herself.'

'That can't be lucky.'

'No, it can't, can it?' Rose says. 'Maybe we should try calling her Ace for now. Can you imagine trying to sell a horse called Maggot? Mares get enough stick as it is.'

'Ace.' I look at the mare, holding her head high out of the window. 'She really is nice,' I say.

'Yeah, luckily for her, or she'd have been given up on by now. Though to be honest, I don't think she's going to be so difficult. She's just lost her way. But she was going around BE100 easily before, so she could go far if we sort things out.'

I shrug. 'She should make someone a nice pony. Is she small enough for pony classes?'

'One-four-nine on the nail. Shod,' Rose says. It is't uncommon for a pony to fail a trot-up because it measures a centimetre over the height limit, and no one goes to try an event pony without taking a reliable measuring stick with them. 'And scope to burn. Or, she did, anyway.'

'She could be an FEI pony, then.'

'She could.' Rose pauses. 'Do you want to help me with her? This summer?'

I look at her. 'Really?'

'Yeah, why not? I mean, I'll check she's not completely nuts, but I don't see why you shouldn't be able to help. I'm a bit big for her, anyway. We could work her together. I'll get her going, and then you can try sitting on her. It'll give you a chance to keep riding this summer, stop you getting bored of fitness work because it does get mind-numbing. What do you think?'

Never in a million years did I think I would be in a position like this. Not riding a pony with all the talent and class to go FEI, or one that is unexperienced and potentially crazy for that matter. I'll be like my friends for once, riding a real contender and not just a low-level schoolmaster. 'I'd love to.'

chapter 4

'So what do you think?' I ask, leaning against the stable door.

Freya nods, looking over her shoulder at the yard. I hand her the body brush in my hand and she passes me a hoof pick and skip without me asking. 'It's nice.' She leans across the half door to scratch Jupiter's neck as I pick up his left fore. 'It seems like a nice place to be.'

'It is,' I say. 'And it will be even better when you have Leo down the road.'

Freya's just returned from Brand Hall, hurrying straight here to see Jupiter and me, and has already filled me in on the day. Leo put in an average dressage and a clear but slow cross country to leave him sitting outside of the top ten going into show jumping tomorrow. There's a chance he'll be long listed, but it's apparently not looking like he'll make the team even if he is, which is good news for Freya.

'Hopefully,' she says, but she doesn't really sound all too hopeful, and when I look up again, putting down Jupiter's foot, her attention is elsewhere. 'Shall I do his tail?' Freya asks, picking a curry comb from my grooming box.

'Sure. You mustn't have groomed a horse in weeks? Not since Diamond left.'

She pulls a dismissive face, letting herself into the stable. 'Nah, I've been helping some friends out with their horses.'

'I was kidding,' I say, though I know Freya will no longer be on the same topic. Freya and I have been best friends for years, crossing paths via ponies, which means I've known her long enough not to take her frequent silences and mood swings seriously. For one thing, she's shy, even around people she knows, and this quietness is often mistaken for arrogance. This isn't helped by Freya being an amazing rider, far better than I'll ever be, which makes the coldness come across as superiority when she's at events. She's also serious, never one to have a laugh when there's a job to be done, and some might find her stuck-up. But my best friend is also one of the kindest people I know, can cheer anyone up, and always puts others before herself. If you'd told me two months ago that this person would sell the pony she'd owned and produced for five years in favour of a schoolmaster that had been on a European team, I would have laughed. I *did* laugh, thought Freya was joking when she told me, but she wasn't, and any attempts on my part to understand exactly how such circumstances came about have been futile.

'I'm really sorry he can't compete,' Freya says to me after a while. She holds Jupiter's tail in her left hand, untangling it to the right, the silver strands accentuating her own red curls - colouring that comes from her Irish father.

I swallow the lump in my throat. 'Yeah, me too. Hey, I haven't told you about Ace yet.'

'Who's Ace?'

While Freya works the comb through Jupiter's tail, I tell her about the mare in as few words as possible, which is still more words than you'd expect considering she's only been at the yard six hours. But in this short time, she's sure made her presence known.

After lunch, once Ace was settled, Rose decided to let her out in the paddock. 'She can relax and familiarise herself with the place,' she said. 'She hasn't been out with others in a little while, so I'll put her out on her own for now.'

Ace walked to the paddock calmly enough, clad in both overreach and tendon boots, and wandered off when Rose unclipped the rope. But then it was like a bomb went off inside her, and she started galloping around, which wasn't particularly out of the ordinary, except that she never stopped. She kept going and going, running along the fence line, letting out the odd whinny.

'She should settle eventually,' Rose said as we watched.

But she didn't, and after a solid hour of full out galloping, Rose was forced to admit defeat and catch the mare before she harmed herself. Or harmed herself *further*, I should say, because she managed to lose two shoes, one leaving a nail sticking out the inside of her foot, pick up a few minor scratches, and looked ready to drop dead of a heart attack.

'It's a vicious circle,' Rose said to me once Ace was back in her stable, dried off, calmly eating hay as though nothing had happened. 'Unless you leave her, she'll never truly settle, but I can't risk her injuring herself, either. Certainly not when she isn't mine. I have to keep going, though, because keeping her in will only make things worse.'

The farrier was texted, though the chances of him

getting here on a weekend are slim, so now we just wait and try it all again tomorrow. At least Ace has good feet, having no difficulty walking over the hard ground even with missing shoes, so she'll still be turned out. If she had more time, Rose said to me while I held the mare's head as she attempted to pull the nail, which was sticking out in such a way that it could easily strike the inside of her right fore, out of Ace's foot, she'd leave her without shoes until she settled in, to avoid unnecessary injuries, but that's not the case, so back on they must go.

'She sounds like a handful,' Freya says.

I straighten up, holding the bucket and hoof pick in my right hand. 'Yeah, but she is really nice. She evented to BE100, and Rose thinks she could go higher. Wanna see her?'

It's evening, but the day shows no signs of ending. June has begun, and night-time is a rare thing that seems to only last the length of a movie. It'll get dark in a few hours, but it's only four in the morning when the sun rises and daylight starts streaming through your windows. Not great when you want to sleep, but very great when you have things called horses to look after.

'Oh, she is nice,' Freya says, sounding surprised. Ace leans over the stable door, ears pricked, and I stop Freya before she holds a hand out.

'Careful. You need to watch her.'

'She bites?'

'Yep.' Something I discovered first-hand today while I was holding her for Rose. 'She can be really sweet, but she can also grab hold of you when you're not expecting it.'

'Do you have an attitude problem?' Freya asks Ace, speaking softly as she approaches the stable door. The mare flickers an ear, unsure, but Freya mumbles words of reassurance, and walks up to her. The pony lowers her head, nothing like the man-eater I just described.

'She likes you,' I say. I don't know why I'm surprised, all horses like Freya.

'She's sweet. Ace did you say her name is?'

I nod. 'Yeah. Though apparently everyone called her Maggot.'

'Well she's certainly not looking like a Maggot now,' comes Rose's voice as she walks up behind us. Freya steps back from the stable door, and Ace regards us a moment before pinning her ears and returning to her hay. 'Oops, spoke too soon. You must be Freya.'

'Freya, this is Rose,' I introduce needlessly.

'Hi Freya,' Rose says. 'It's so nice to meet you.'

'You too,' Freya says, always polite.

'So you've tamed our beast?' Rose goes on, stepping up to Ace.

Freya shrugs. 'She doesn't seem so bad.'

'No, she doesn't,' Rose agrees. A hint of jealously flickers inside me, as much as I will it not to. Of course Freya's better with horses than I am, I know that, and of course she's the one getting the ready-made FEI pony, and of *course* the pony I have to school prefers her. I've always felt like I have to work and fight to the bone for the things others seem to achieve easily. Freya and I might have been eventing at the same level up to now, but I've been doing so on a schoolmaster, while she took a hundred pound youngster up the ranks all on her own. 'I think I've seen you ride past often. A spotted pony?

Freya nods. 'Yes, Diamond. He just went to a new home last month.'

Mention of a sold pony pulses fear through me, remembering how secret the whole Leo thing is right now, and if Rose says something, then Freya will think *I* said something, even though it wasn't even my fault. 'He was lovely,' Rose says, which makes Freya flick her eyes away - only noticeable because I'm looking for a reaction. 'Well if you want something to ride while you look for your next project, don't hesitate to stop by. There's always a horse to take out.' Rose looks at me quickly, silent reassurance, and I smile back.

'Thank you, that's really nice of you.'

'I mean it,' Rose says, and remembering her daughter's insistence earlier, which was maybe nothing but generosity, I think that the apple doesn't fall far from the tree. 'Anytime.'

'Thank you,' Freya says again. 'I will, if I get a chance.'

Nothing more is said of bought or sold ponies, and instead Rose walks us around the yard, introducing Freya and me to her string of horses. There's Sterling, her former three-star ride who now earns his keep being ridden in the odd lesson, and Sunny, a beautiful six-year-old warmblood with a dark brown coat, as well as a few other youngsters she has in for schooling, but it's a more experienced horse that catches Freya's eye.

'He's gorgeous,' she says enthusiastically, stepping up to the gelding's stable door. 'I love chestnuts.'

'You're not the only one I know,' Rose says, smiling to herself. 'This here is Paddington,' she goes on, introducing the chestnut in question. 'Nobody really thought much of him as a youngster, and he was only supposed to be a quick resale project, not thinking he'd go any higher than Novice, but every question I presented him with he just kept on answering, and now's he's going around two-star and

Intermediate, and I'm aiming for Blenheim at the end of the year. He's one you could hack out, if you wanted. Safe as houses.'

Mum and Nell - Freya's mum - arrive while we're still cooing over the chestnut gelding. Nell is exactly as you'd expect Freya's mum to be - kind, polite, caring - but without quite the same amount of shyness. While she doesn't ride, Nell works as a racing secretary in Newmarket, and her husband for one of the horse transport companies. Mum's probably spent more time in the saddle than the two of them combined, and yet sometimes I wish I had parents who were involved with horses the same way, who lived in the world day-to-day, and then immediately feel bad about it. I can't say Mum is any stricter than Nell, even if she is more likely to say the wrong thing at exactly the right time, and wouldn't take out a loan just to buy me an FEI pony.

Everyone chats for what feels like a short while but my watch reveals to be an hour, discussing everything from eventing to the willow tree outside Freya's house to what cake flavours Mum will be serving in the café. Then Mackenzie comes out of the house with the two puppies - Flopsy and Florence - and we fuss over them until we realise that daylight has faded and we're all standing in the dark. There's a rush of hurrying around to finish what yard chores are left, Mum, Nell, and Freya adamant to help, and then we all walk home, heading to our respective dwellings on the same country road, and I decide that this change could turn out to be all right after all.

'One cappuccino and one slice of lemon drizzle cake comes to five pounds twenty, please,' I say, tapping the till.

This is my first morning in the café, and I have to say

that I like it. The walls look beige to me but Mum calls them taupe, adorned with framed photos of racehorses on the gallops. There's an assortment of seating areas, from single areas to sit with a laptop, to armchairs and coffee tables for larger groups. The counter is a large glass case of goodies - croissants, slices of cheesecake, crumbly cookies - beyond which it turns into a table with stools, and behind the till the menu is written out in chalk. There's one full-time barista, as well as a couple of people in the kitchen, and then Mum. As nice a place as it is, it also seems like a lot of work, something I've never really noticed until today. I'm surprised Mum is as calm as she has been, considering this all rests on her shoulders.

'You managing?' she says to me now, watching as the last customer carries their coffee and cake to a table.

I nod. 'Think so. It's not too busy.'

'Doesn't look like Mondays are,' Mum agrees. 'Thank you,' she adds.

'It's fine.' School starts again tomorrow, and then the countdown to summer begins. The schedule I had a few weeks ago, plans to compete Jupi all summer, has been thrown overboard, and I'm not holding my breath that Ace will be capable of anything anytime soon, even if Rose were to allow me to compete her. She isn't ours, after all, and she'll be sold anyway, as soon as a buyer comes along.

'Wow, this place is amazing!'

Speaking of. Rose walks up to the counter, her smile wide as she takes in the interior of the café, glass door swinging shut behind her. It's nearing lunchtime, so she must have just finished riding, dressed in jodhpurs and boots.

'Rose!' Mum says brightly, walking around the side of the counter. 'What a nice surprise! There're still a few things that need finishing, but we're getting there…'

'I love it. I really do. Gosh, I admire you.' She looks around, shaking her head in disbelief. 'I could never achieve anything like this. It's fantastic.'

'There are some changes I need to make,' Mum says again. 'I really want it to be a place that both encompasses racing and is somewhere all those involved with the horses want to come, but also appeal to people who want to sit and work or read. I was thinking of building up a library wall, over there, that people can take and leave from.'

'I love that idea. And I'm sure Ben has a box of books or two to spare, because we have more than we can fit in the house. Perils of marrying a lit teacher,' she adds. 'I'm not joking when I say we own seven copies of *War and Peace.*'

'Would you like a drink?' I ask.

'On the house,' Mum adds adamantly.

'Ooh, a coffee with milk would be great. Whatever coffee shops call those now.' Rose walks up to the counter, balancing on one of the stools. 'I'm not often passing through town, so I thought I should stop by while I was here.'

'I'm glad you did,' Mum says, walking behind the counter to start making the coffee. 'You heading somewhere.'

'The horse feed place. Our little pony' - she looks at me - 'is still turning her nose up at everything, and she doesn't eat much when she does, so I'm going to try haylage, and get a bag of rice pellets to put in her feed, and maybe even try another more fattening mix, too. The excitement of horses.'

'You should go, Sybil,' Mum says to me. 'Rose is kind enough to let you help with this horse, the least you could do is help back.'

Other than hold Ace while Rose pulled the nail out of her foot, I've haven't done anything remotely "helpful" yet. She was turned out in the paddock again yesterday, on her own to see if the day before was just a one off, which only resulted in another lost shoe and running off even more weight she couldn't afford to lose.

'Don't *you* need my help?' I ask Mum, hoping she'll take the hint. I'm sure the last thing Rose wants is to be stuck babysitting me.

'No, no, go!'

'It's not very interesting, but you're more than welcome to come,' Rose says.

And like that I'm sitting in the passenger seat of Rose's four-by-four, driving towards the feed store. The vehicle probably hasn't been cleaned in my lifetime. The dashboard is covered in dust, every footwell piled up with buckets and head collars and enough horse equipment to make you think that Rose has to drive to her horses every day and doesn't have them right on her doorstep. The car also makes me feel at ease right away.

'The farrier's coming this afternoon to do Ace,' Rose tells me as we slow to let some racehorses cross the road. Three Thoroughbreds walk across the tarmac, some of the last of the day, shaking their heads with annoyance. Three thousand horses in a town of fifteen thousand people. I don't follow racing, and even I recognise some of the jockeys and trainers I pass on the streets. 'Whether or not she keeps them on is another matter.'

'At least you'll be able to work her.'

Rose nods, the car cruising along again as the horses safely reach the pavement. 'I might leave her tonight if she's only being shod this afternoon, but I'll get her on the lunge tomorrow and see what we're dealing with. The Matthewses supposedly had her working for a few weeks, under saddle in the school, but we'll see. I'll stick a saddle on her if she's all right, and maybe just try walking her around. And if you're up for it, you can start riding her once I've got her going.'

'Yeah, if I'm good enough.'

'Sure you are. You never know, you might even get a round or two on her before she's sold. *Sybil Young and Ace of Hearts are clear to the last,*' she says in a commentator's voice.

'Dawson,' I correct automatically.

'Yes, of course.' Rose looks embarrassed by the mistake. 'I should've assumed your mum's using her maiden name.'

I shake my head. 'She isn't. Young is her married name, but my dad - who I call my dad - isn't really my father.' I'm not sure why I'm telling Rose this, when I usually avoid getting into the confusion that is my family tree, but I go on. 'My mum and my real dad split up before I was born, but I still have his last name. Mum married who I call my dad, Gabe's dad, a couple of years later, and they both have his last name. It's a bit confusing,' I add, embarrassed.

'No, not at all.' A pause. 'Do you see much of your real dad?'

'Not really. He's been living in Canada for the past ten years, so other than the two phone calls a year - Christmas and my birthday - we don't really speak.'

'How do you and Gabe get along?' Rose asks, changing the subject.

'Good. Even though he's not interested in horses, we still have things in common. We bicker a bit, but not much. We all get along, really. Or at least we did.' I look down at my lap, at the dust and crumbs wedged along the stitching of the seat. 'Mum and Dad never argued. Ever. So it never occurred to either of us that anything like this would happen.'

'Things aren't always as they appear,' Rose says cautiously. 'Sometimes people are very good at hiding their worries from others. Or maybe they loved you both too much to ever let things get to the arguing stage. But it must be tough.'

I shrug. 'People go through worse.'

Rose slows as we come to a red light, and I crane my neck to see up the driveway beside us, one leading into a racing yard.

'I don't have any brothers or sisters,' Rose says after a moment. 'And growing up, my parents had every reason to be happy. But they argued all the time. Every evening, without fail. They looked after me, but they were horrid to each other. It's probably why I wound up working with horses, because I spent all my time at the stables. It was like they were staying together for me, when really I would have given anything for them to split up, so that they could be happy, and I could enjoy each of my parents without the anger.'

'Did they?' I ask. 'Ever split up?'

'Not until it was too late.' The light turns green, and Rose lowers her foot on the accelerator. 'It might not seem like it now, but maybe your parents splitting up was them doing the most selfless thing they could, by making sure you and Gabe never had to experience the two of them arguing.'

'Maybe.' My eyes flicker to Rose, whose life seems so perfect. She may not be rich, or living what some people consider to be the high life, but she is happy, and doing what she loves, with a family to support her. And yet it wasn't always that way. 'I'm not always a fan of things changing,' I admit.

'Who is? But if you don't go through the bad changes, you'll never experience a good one.'

It's at four o'clock the next afternoon that I walk into the yard tired from the first day back at school. Gabe and I took the bus to Cambridge this morning, which we'll be doing every weekday for the next month and a half, until summer holidays, with the intention of transferring to Newmarket in September. While I don't mind my school, there isn't anyone I'm upset to leave, especially since I'll be with Freya after the summer, and Gabe's feelings about the situation fall somewhere between ecstasy and dread. He's never made friends easily, despite being the nicest anyone could have, and has always been an easy target for bullies. The chance to start over is also a chance for things to be even worse.

I see Jupiter, grazing happily in his paddock, but first I see Rose, leading a certain bay mare to the sand school. She raises a hand when she sees me, an action that, surprisingly enough, makes Ace come to a standstill, halting with her front feet together. For such a strong-willed animal, a mind that is hers and only hers, I've noticed in the past few days that she's both responsive and well-mannered. Her owners neglected to tell Rose that she's difficult to shoe, though, because nailing shoes onto her feet somewhat correctly was all the farrier could manage yesterday, while Rose held the rearing mare, and I tried treating her as a distraction, but she was too stubborn to take anything from me. Early this morning she was turned out in the pony field, with Jupiter,

Cinder, and Jemima's roan, Pheasant, and it was a pleasant surprise when she acted submissively and settled to graze within minutes.

'Hey,' Rose greets me. 'Perfect timing. How was school? Now, tell me, I don't suppose *you* tied yourself to your staircase with scarves this morning to try to get out of going?'

What? 'Um, no...' *Wait.* 'No, really?'

Rose nods slowly, her face amused and tired. 'Mackenzie tied herself to the staircase. She made Jemima help her, too. Worst thing is it took me and Ben ten minutes to get the knots undone and the kids *did* end up being late for school.' I laugh, unable to help it. 'At lest Ben takes them,' Rose goes on. 'I think I'd have lost my patience. I'm so bad at the whole school run thing. I have to pick up or drop off occasionally, and I just can't do it.' She shakes her head. 'I was waiting for Mima once some years ago, and one of the other mothers started talking to me about all these classes her kid was taking, and how they were heading to aerobics that evening and what not, and she asked me what Jemima did. And I was like, "She's six, she can go outside and play with a stick!". And I actually did say that, I'm not kidding, and none of those mothers have ever looked at me again.'

'Mum would never make me and Gabe go to extra activities, either. I was allowed to start riding because I drove her mad asking, and Gabe's never been interested in anything other than reading, really.'

'And the two of you will be better off because of it. Though, based on the knots I had to undo this morning, maybe my kids *should* be attending Brownies. Isn't that all about learning to tie knots?'

'They have horses,' I say. 'Don't we all excel at tying

knots?'

'Fair point. In which case, you'd think I'd have been better at untying them. Anyway.' Rose nods to Ace beside her. 'This girl was a pleasure to tack up. I was only trying saddles to see which fits her best, but she was so unbothered that I just went ahead and left it on her. Funny, the difficult ones are often good about things like that, and yet it's the more placid horses who freak out after a bit of time off. Not that she's been off for more than a week, but still. Shall we see what we're dealing with?'

I sit on a filler by the railings as Rose leads Ace to the middle of the school. The mare is in an all-purpose saddle, a worn Stübben, over a navy blue saddle cloth. Her bridle is old, reins twisted and with the throat lash passed through one of the loops, securing them. Ace's expression is alert, curious, accentuating the dish of her head, her little ears pricked. She really is beautiful.

'I haven't put side reins on because I want to see how she is first,' Rose explains, re-winding the lunge line into her right hand and putting a whip down at her feet. Even though she's on the ground, Rose wears a skullcap, her calves clad in worn chaps.

'She looks nice.'

'Don't speak too soon.'

The bay mare walks a circle around Rose, staying in a relaxed rhythm, but her ears and eyes suggest otherwise. Like she's ready to run away at any moment. Her ribcage shows through her shiny coat, but even though she's thin, Ace looks fit. The Thoroughbred in her shows in her shape, in the slope of her shoulder and the angle of her croup. Her neck comes out of her shoulder at exactly the right point - not too low, putting her on the forehand, neither too high to make her look like a giraffe. A real event horse.

'Trot on,' Rose says after a while, clicking her tongue. Ace springs forward with a shake of her head, and for a moment I think she's going to take off, about to explode, but she doesn't. The mare moves on, ducking her head again, and flies into an extended trot, tucking her nose to her chest. Rose whoas her, lifting the lunge, and after a few strides, Ace slows her rhythm, coming up off the forehand, and falls into a perfect trot. There's a soft arch to her neck, the curve beneath her jaw a perfect upside down U, the front of her head perpendicular to the ground. Her hind feet land on the tracks left by the front in the sand, her body working as a whole. She looks like a pony about to go into an FEI test.

'Wow,' I say.

Rose smiles, keeping her eyes on the mare. 'Nice, isn't she? Just as nice as I remember. Can't say she'll be the same under saddle, though. But I tell you, if she were a hand or two bigger…'

After a few minutes on this rein, incorporating transitions back to walk, Rose unclips the lunge line to attach it on the opposite side, running it through one snaffle ring and attaching it to the other, turning Ace onto the right rein. The bay is just as balanced on this rein as the other, moving with impulsion and grace, her hooves floating across the sand. To think *I* might get a chance to ride this horse…

'Well, I daresay everything's looking too simple.' Rose brings Ace to a halt and walks across the circle to greet her. Ace tilts her head to the side, her right eye following Rose's every move. There's something about the way she carries herself, the way she regards everything and everyone around her, that makes me think Ace believes that all she is doing, she is doing because *she* has decided to, not because she is being told to. 'I guess there's nothing left to do but get on.'

'You're going to ride her?' I stand up from my seat and walk towards Rose. She passes me the rolled up lunge line, the action watched closely by Ace, and undoes the throat lash to free the reins.

'Only a few minutes, to see how she is. I should know quickly enough what I'm dealing with. Would you hold the stirrup for me?'

I walk around to Ace's right side, her nostrils twitching as I do, and pull the stirrup down, holding on to the leather. Rose practises jumping up and down beside the mare a few times, purposely making her actions brisk, tapping the saddle with her hand. When Ace doesn't move, just flickers her ears, Rose nods at me, a sign, and puts her foot to the stirrup. Smaller than her usual rides, she easily makes the height with little effort, managing to lift her right leg over the saddle and lower her seat without putting any weight on the pony's back. I release the leather as Rose's foot finds the stirrup, step back out of the way. Ace hasn't moved, standing stock-still, her expression the only thing showing that she's aware of what's going on. Rose settles into the saddle, moving slightly to find her comfortable balance, before rising into a two-point seat and clicking her tongue, hands resting against Ace's neck. The mare hesitates, but Rose clicks her tongue again and she takes a step forward. Ace looks the same as she did on the lunge - athletic, elegant, wary. After a few strides, Rose sits in the saddle, seat visibly loosening, and the mare's body tenses a moment, only to relax again.

'A bit cold-backed,' Rose comments. 'She saw an osteo

last month and was fine, so it's just something we'll have to work on. Horses generally misbehave for two reasons: pain or fear. She's been checked for pain in the past - back, teeth, saddle. So you know the problems you're left with are behavioural. But you can't correct any of that until you take away the pain.'

Back from my spot at the railings, I watch Rose walk Ace around. She circles, frequently changing rein, asking Ace to soften into the hand. The mare looks great, and soon Rose is easing her into a trot. Ace starts off quicker than she did on the lunge, rushing, but Rose settles her. This is the first time I've seen her ride in the flesh, other than the few cross country pictures in the tack room, all of Sterling and Paddington, and I'm more than a little impressed. It's not that she's stylish and effective, even though she's both, but how she manages to adapt to Ace so quickly, how she gets the best out of her. It's not long until the little mare is trotting beautifully around the school, nothing like the wild horse my mind has concocted since she arrived.

'How does she feel?' I ask Rose when she comes back to walk.

'Okay,' she says, letting the reins out to pat the mare on the neck. 'She obviously tries to run away from the leg, and she fakes the contact into the hand - especially on the left because she doesn't go into the right rein - but I'm sure she could be wonderful. On the flat, anyway. Do you want a sit?'

'Me?' I stare dumbly. The last thing I expected today was to ride Ace myself. 'You sure?'

Rose nods. 'Just a couple of circles to see how you feel. If you don't interfere, I'm confident she won't do anything. You know what they say: tell a gelding, ask a mare. Just don't *tell* her. I also think that geldings are dogs and mares are cats. I'll walk her while you grab your hat.'

When I come back from the tack room with my hat and chaps, Rose is holding Ace in the middle of school, shortening the stirrups. I jog a few steps, not wanting to keep her waiting, and climb through the railings with butterflies in my stomach. I'm actually going to ride this beautiful, well-schooled horse. I've never ridden a horse that does flatwork as well as that before.

'Ready?' says Rose. 'Do you want me to hold the stirrup or give you a leg-up?'

'Stirrup,' I say. I've never been able to get the hang of leg-ups.

Rose holds the stirrup with her left hand and Ace's reins with her right. The mare eyes me suspiciously as I approach her, and I rub her neck in reassurance, though she doesn't care for the show of affection. I gather the reins and raise my foot to the stirrup, imagining how riding Ace will be. She looked so amazing, so quiet in the mouth…

Ace fidgets when I settle into the saddle, not how she was with Rose, and I shorten my reins, make sure I have control. Rose finds my foot with the right stirrup, keeping hold of the reins.

'You okay?'

I nod, trying to shake away the nerves. 'Yep.'

'All right. I'll let go, and you can just let her walk on a circle around me. You might feel like her back comes up beneath you, and if you get worried just stand in your stirrups a few strides until she settles. Just ride soft and you'll be fine.'

I touch my legs to Ace's sides. The mare shuffles forward, head coming up, and I feel what Rose said, like her spine is curving upwards beneath the saddle, but it passes just as quickly. As I move onto a circle, as Ace walks on beneath me, I feel a lump of fear lodge itself in my chest. She feels nothing like how I expected her to. With Rose on her back, Ace looked impeccably schooled, almost easy to ride, with a lovely, soft head carriage. But she feels nothing like that at all. She's a nice size, maybe a little narrow, with the right amount of neck and shoulder in front of the saddle but I feel like I'm just balanced on her, not safe in the saddle, as though I could bounce off - or be thrown off - at any moment. Everything's so different from Jupiter. Every action, however small, Ace reacts to. I can't move an inch without her interpreting the movement. Like sitting on half a ton of fire and attitude.

'Keep walking on a circle around me,' Rose says. 'Sit up tall, keep your seat soft, and just gently coax her to go down. Keep your outside hand steady, pushing her into it with your inside leg.'

I want to say that I can't, that there's no way I can manage any of this, but I do what Rose says, just as though I were warming Jupiter up for dressage, and am surprised when Ace responds immediately, ducking her head and walking on into the hand.

'There you go, perfect.'

'That's it?' I say. Surely it can't be that easy? What horse walks through their back, into the hand, perfectly on the bridle, in a matter of seconds? *One that is correctly schooled,* I tell myself. 'She's working from behind?'

Rose nods. 'Yep. She goes well on the flat. Change rein across the circle when you like.'

For a few minutes, I walk Ace around Rose, the mare staying round and collected. I can't stop grinning. It's amazing to ride a horse that doesn't resist the contact, doesn't fight to not go in the right shape. Is this how everyone else's horses feel?

'Do you want to try a trot before we call it a day?'

I nod, excited at the prospect. At the next corner, I ask Ace for a transition the same way I would Jupiter, but the mare shoots away from my aids, rushing with her head in the air, and it takes me a moment to find my balance, to adjust to her stride.

'Whoa, steady,' Rose says. 'You don't need to be strong with her, you just need to ask. Sit softly, I shouldn't be able to hear your seat land in the saddle when you rise, and just let your body relax.'

How I'm supposed to relax when the horse beneath me is doing everything to make sure I can't I don't know. I can't get my leg on, can't find the balance to rise the trot without hitting the saddle, and all this just makes Ace more annoyed. She's rushing, making me feel even more unsteady, and everything I do just seems to make it worse.

'Slow her,' Rose says softly. 'Circle her around me and just slow her right down, with the outside rein, until you can get your balance. When you do, she'll soften.'

I find that hard to believe, but I don't have a choice unless I want to stay up here forever, so I do my best to slow Ace, around Rose, and after a while the mare's stride slows, her rhythm easier to sit, and she even lowers her head for a few seconds, but I can't feel a thing in either rein, so I know it's not my doing.

'Good girl. Leave her on that, come back to walk.'

Happily. There's no working on the transition today, just going from trot to walk, and Ace shortens her body, the way she did when I got on. I stand in the stirrups, and she jogs a stride before settling, a terrifying moment during which I think she'll take off.

'Well done,' Rose says to me. 'You did good. She's not easy.'

'She's different from Jupiter,' I say, taking my feet out of the stirrups as Ace halts.

'Very. But this could be good for you, because it'll teach you to ride something sensitive. And you'll get a feel for what flatwork should be like, and then you can apply it to Jupi.'

My feet find the ground, which feels very good, and I pat Ace on the neck, making sure I reward her. She keeps her gaze directed forward, but the mare also watches me from the corner of her eye, ears back, teeth clenched. I'm not sure I even want to sit on this horse again, let alone school it. What have I got myself into?

chapter 5

Gabe comes back from walking the dogs with a pile of books in his arms so high that I'm surprised they're still balanced. It's hard enough not being knocked over by Frodo when that's all you have to think about.

'Look,' he says, dumping them onto the kitchen table, letting go of the dogs. The leads make a noise as they're dragged across the floor, plastic handles rattling, and I unclip them, seeing as Gabe isn't about to.

Our house isn't large. The opposite, even. The front door opens into the living room, which consists of a sitting area on the left, a table in the middle, and then leads into an open kitchen, nestled into the right-hand corner. It's an old building with new-enough amenities, comfortable. The windows at the back of the house look out on to the garden we seldom step foot in. A staircase next to the kitchen leads upstairs, where there are three small bedrooms - I can cross mine in two steps - and a bathroom that rarely runs hot water for more than eight minutes.

'Close the door, Gabe,' Mum says as the dogs edge

dangerously close. She's doing accounts at the table, and Gabe's books have unsettled her system.

My brother obliges, closing the door before a dog can escape onto the road, and resumes his chatter. 'I found a phone box library!' he says excitedly. 'Just down the road. It has *tons* of books, and loads I want to read but haven't. Look!'

I look through the books absently, most of them fantasy authors we've read before. Megan Whalen Turner, Robin Mckinley, W. J. Heathcote, Garth Nix...

'I think you're only supposed to take one at a time and leave a book in exchange,' Mum points out.

'I'll take them back when I've read them,' Gabe mumbles, picking up a book and flipping to the first page, as though he's about to start reading it this very second. He probably is.

I tap one of the well-worn paperbacks on the table. 'Save that one for me.' I've just come back from the yard, having ridden Jupiter in walk and watched Rose lunge Ace, who I've only sat on a couple of times since our first ride and to little improvement. I only ran back for a snack, because there's somewhere I want to be. 'I'm going to Freya's, I'll be back later.'

'He's gorgeous.'

My arms are over the paddock railing, my chin resting on them as I stare enviously at the pony grazing in the field. He's fourteen-two on the nail, but he could pass for a horse from a distance. His condition is immaculate, his body nothing but lean muscle. His summer coat is a vibrant red, glimmering like wax in the warm evening sun, and his equally red tail looks like silk. His mane is pulled to perfection, only just falling over the crest of his neck as he snatches at the grass. There's a white star in the centre of his forehead, and when he looks up, his head is elegantly dished, nose dark. Farther along from the pony a couple of rabbits are dozing, ears flat against their backs.

'He's settled really well,' Freya says, waving her hand as a fly settles on her cheek. 'I was worried he wouldn't, on his own, but he can see the horses across the road.'

Leo is in one of Freya's two paddocks. It's one field, really, just with a fence running down the middle to separate it into two grazing parcels, each one an acre. Between the paddocks, near the house, is a wooden stable block, the sort that can be bought as a kit, which is two stables but used as one as there's no partition. It has two doors, though, and Freya simply opens the one whichever side of the paddock a pony is turned out in, closing the other, so that it's a shelter they can access at any time. A plastic tarpaulin covers hay and straw on pallets beside the stable block, bins contain feed, and a big plastic box intended for pool accessories houses rugs, with a grooming box by the stable door. Freya keeps all of her tack in the house, for fear of theft, and carries the saddle and bridle out every day to ride.

'Have you ridden him yet?'

She shakes her head, pulling a face. 'He only arrived this afternoon. I'll give him the day to settle, maybe tomorrow too, and then take him for a hack.'

I'd be too afraid to ride a new pony for the first time on a hack, going off alone along the road, but Freya isn't like that. Then again, Battersea isn't just any pony, either. An unlucky two rails at the Pony Championships at Brand Hall dropped him down the order and he didn't make the long list for Europeans, much to Freya's delight. Who could blame her, owning a pony like this. Leo's been in a British squad, after all, and at thirteen years of age, he still has time to be again.

'Hi Sybil,' comes Nell's voice as she walks out of the house, Stripes the impeccably behaved Dalmatian at her heels. The thatch cottage is only a few feet from the road, but it makes up for this with the few acres of land that stretches out behind it. In addition to the paddocks, there's a well-kept fenced garden and an open piece of land that Freya uses for schooling. And then, the house's namesake, a gigantic willow tree whose branches Freya and I have frequently swung from, standing proud beside the white building. 'Getting acquainted with Leo?'

'He's so gorgeous,' I say. I glance at Freya, but she's looking away, much less excited than I am, and focusses on fussing over Stripes. How is that possible? How can she not be jumping out of her skin because this incredible one-star pony is hers?

'How's Jup doing?' Nell asks. Freya might get her red hair from her father, but everything else comes from her mum. The thick curls, the strong jaw, the dark brown eyes, the tall, lean figure. They have the same calm way of speaking, except Freya occasionally echoes her father's Irish accent. Nell is older than Mum, and it shows in some ways, but she's also more active and able.

'He's good. Still only walking him, but he'll start working in trot next week.'

'And that little mare? You liked her, didn't you, Freya?'

Well you can't have her because you already have the best pony in the whole of freaking England, I think bitterly. I'm sure Freya has some remorse about selling Diamond, her self-produced pony, even if she hasn't voiced anything to me, but she could look a little more excited. And it's not her fault Ace likes her better than she likes me, I remind myself. 'She's doing okay,' I tell Nell. 'I've ridden her a few times, but Rose has been mainly lunging her. I haven't jumped her or anything,' I add. 'Only walked and trotted. She's cold-backed, and Rose wants her to get stronger before we do too much more.'

'Very sensible,' Nell says. 'I like Rose. Maybe you should think about trying a lesson with her on Leo, Freya.'

'Maybe,' Freya says with a shrug. With Diamond, in addition to attending clinics, she went for a monthly private lesson with the European pony team coach, which I presumed she'd be doing even more with Leo. Part of me hopes she will, and not come to Rose's, because then I'll only look like an even worse rider. Whenever we ride together in public, at events or clinics, everyone is always telling Freya - or Nell - what an amazing rider she is, how natural her position is, what a good eye for a stride she has. They never say the opposite to me, just don't say anything at all, and I wish I could just get one compliment, one word of praise, to stop feeling like such a failure compared to everyone else. Proving myself to Rose is a chance to achieve that, but it'll never happen if Freya's in the picture.

'I'd better get back,' I say. 'Mum told me not to be too long.'

'Say hi to her for me,' Nell says. 'Come by anytime. You girls should be able to go riding together soon.'

I nod. 'Yep.'

'I'll call you tomorrow if I don't see you,' Freya says. We talked on the phone all the time when I lived in Cambridge, too far away to see each other more than once a week, and even though there's only a lane between us now, it's a habit we can't seem to break.

'Me too.'

'Do you want a lift?' Nell asks.

'No, it's fine. I might stop by the yard again, too.'

As I walk down the lane, I stop to look back behind me. The higgledy-piggledy thatch cottage, the big sweeping willow tree, and just a glimpse of a chestnut pony in the back paddock. From the outside, it all looks perfect, and I wonder what the view from the inside is like.

Jupiter bobs his head up and down, using my shoulder as a scratching post, and I give him a tight smile. 'You're my number one,' I tell him, running my index finger down the front of his head. 'If only you were fit and sound, and we could ride and compete all summer. I'd much rather ride you than that mad thing,' I add, then immediately feel guilty. No one is making me ride Ace, after all. Rose is trying to help, offering me a pony to school since I can't do much with my own, and I was excited to ride her before I knew how much of an amateur I would feel like on her. Seeing Leo yesterday hasn't helped, only made me feel worse. If only I could have a pony like that. Instead I have one that's unsound physically and the other mentally. Nothing in life is fair.

'Hey, I didn't see you arrive,' Rose says, coming up to the stable door. She has her riding kit on and a bridle across her shoulder, so she must be about to work Ace - her competition string get worked in the morning, and she waits for me to exercise the mare.

I nod. 'Yep. Mum dropped me and Gabe off, so I was going to walk him again. Unless you need the school,' I add.

'Actually, this is perfect. I really think Ace needs to get out of the school, so why don't we go for a hack together?

Just a walk around the block. Do them both the world of good.'

'Okay,' I say, trying to muster more enthusiasm than I feel.

The truth is, while I tell people that Jupiter isn't great to hack alone, he isn't great to hack full stop. He jigs and pulls at the bit, and it makes me nervous. The only horse he's ever been good to ride with is Diamond, Freya's old pony, which is why I've always wanted to live near her. Jupiter and Diamond have been to so many shows together, so many clinics, and Freya and I even took them to the beach once. Diamond's a calming influence, which, somehow, I fear Ace isn't going to be.

'Wow, he's looking good,' Rose says when I lead Jupiter out of his stable. And I can't disagree. Advised by Rose, his haynets have doubled in size since coming here, and rather than make him fat it's had the opposite effect. He's still chunky - he's a Connemara, he always will be - but his stomach has lost the bulge it used to have. His feed has changed too, the scoop of pony nuts and alfalfa now accompanied by bran and sugar beet, which Rose swears is better for his system.

'A pony that is naturally chunky like him will store food if he's not getting enough,' she said. 'All horses need to eat. By giving him the right amount of hay, you won't be fattening him up but helping his digestion. Horses should have unlimited hay.'

'He is,' I agree now, stepping back to look at my pony. He looks healthy, proportionate, no one part of his body standing out more than another. The combination of summer and good food has brought out his dapples, covering his rump like a blanket. 'So's she,' I say, nodding at

87

Ace. She's still lean, much leaner than Jupiter, but she's not as ribby as she was when she arrived, and what she does lack in weight she makes up for in coat, her dark body putting Jupiter's dapples to shame.

'We're getting there,' Rose says, swinging lightly into the saddle. 'Are you happy to go onto bridle paths? I know some people feel safer sticking to roads, but I prefer getting to grass.'

Who in their right mind feels safer riding a horse on a road? 'That's fine,' I say.

Rose takes Ace on ahead, looking very relaxed for somebody hacking a supposedly mad horse for the first time. The change of scenery baffles Jupiter too much for him to misbehave, and he follows calmly, my ears filled only with the sound of his and Ace's shod hooves hitting the road, a consistent rhythm, until we turn off onto a grass track, before reaching Freya's house. To her credit Ace looks very quiet, almost... *happy,* her ears forward, delicate head moving with her neck as Rose lets her walk on a loose rein, eyes alight. The mare shows no sign of wanting to take off, of being anxious. As for my pony, however, the steady cadence we have on the road is short-lived. Once he has all four feet on the grass bridle path, Jupiter flips a switch. He decides that the wide track can't be for anything but galloping, and bounds into a prance. I try to slow him, try to stop him before Ace notices, but my attempts only make him worse. In the moment of trying to steady Jupiter, I've taken my leg off, and I try to put it back on, but I may as well try saddling a bird.

'You okay?' Rose asks, looking back over her shoulder.

No, I think, but I don't want her to see me panic. 'I'm fine,' I say, struggling to get the words out as I hold on to the pony. He's rocking back and forth now, trying to take off. 'He just gets excited on hacks.'

Rose halts Ace - because of course even Ace can halt on a hack - resting a hand on her thigh as she watches Jupiter. 'Do you want to try taking him in front? That might settle in him.'

I clear the lump in my throat. 'I'll try. It doesn't usually work…'

I edge Jupiter around Ace, to the front of her, but he's still moving sideways, pulling my arms out. Even as my attention is fully on not falling off, I glance back at Ace, making sure I haven't set her off, but she isn't the least bit bothered.

'See if you can keep your leg on him,' Rose coaches me, walking Ace a few strides behind, to Jupiter's side so that I can see her. 'Get him thinking, using his brain, so he can't mess around. Ask him for a shoulder-in down here, a half-pass - anything to distract him.'

I try to school Jupiter, to ask him to execute dressage movements, but my legs have turned to spaghetti, and he knows it. Nothing I do is working, and he's just getting more and more worked up. As if being taken off with isn't bad enough, the last thing he needs is a wild gallop, because that's definitely not part of his rehab programme.

'He's go… going to take off,' I stammer, fighting tears as Jupiter wrenches the reins from my hands to put his head between his legs.

'He won't, I won't let him,' Rose says, voice steady and reassuring. 'If for a single moment you think he's about to take off, you turn him into Ace, okay? Use her as your barrier.'

The thought of voluntarily crashing into Ace is even

more terrifying than being tanked with into the distance. But then Jupiter leaps, taking all the last strength in my arms with him, and I close my eyes, knowing I have no control. Except he stops.

'That's enough,' Rose says, and I open my eyes to see Ace, right up against Jupiter, with Rose leaning to the side, holding on to Jupiter's head, fingers grasping the rein buckle attached to the ring of his snaffle bit.

The short moment of thinking I was about to be thrown off has made the tears I've been fighting fall freely down by face, and I bite my lip to keep any more from making an appearance. 'I'm sorry,' I say, wiping my eyes with my sleeve. 'When he does that, I don't know what to do.' I look at Ace, patiently putting up with Jupiter's head against her neck, not the least bit perturbed.

Rose looks at me, her eyes going from my tear-stained face to the wound-up pony. 'Get off,' she says.

'What?'

But Rose has already taken her feet from Ace's stirrups, swinging to the ground. 'Get off. He can't pull you around like that.'

Only too happy to get off, I take my feet out of the stirrups and jump to the grass. 'Shall I lead him back?' I ask.

'No, no, I'll ride him, you get on Ace.'

'What?' Jupiter isn't sounding like the worst option anymore.

'You'll be fine,' Rose says. 'Trust me, this mare loves being out. Her problems are in a school, not out of it. I'll help you up, come on.'

Rose is waiting, holding both ponies - Jupiter tilting his head and trying to walk into her, Ace standing calmly - and for fear of causing more trouble, I raise my left foot to the stirrup and settle onto the mare's back. She still feels wrong. Too narrow, too uptight, too ready to throw me on the ground. But surely Rose wouldn't have made me get on if she were about to do anything crazy.

Jupiter moves when Rose gathers the reins in her left hand, pinning his ears as he sidesteps, and she growls at him. 'Pack it in, that's enough.' Her voice is calm and firm, and the pony stops his fidgeting long enough for her to swing a leg over and settle in the saddle. 'Do you need to shorten your stirrups?' she asks me.

'I'm okay.' They could do with being one hole shorter, but they're short enough. And I'd rather they be a bit long than try to adjust them now.

'All right. You go on ahead, make sure you're comfortable, and we'll walk beside you.'

'Are *you* okay?' I ask, watching Jupiter shake his head and jig on the spot with annoyance. It's weird to not only see Rose on my pony, but see anyone on him. I'm always the one riding, always in the saddle myself, and I never get to see what he looks like with a rider, because under saddle is a lot different from standing on his own. Looking at him now, I see what Rose saw before. His body is a natural arch, but not the right way up. He's chunky, but he doesn't carry himself correctly, his back end lacking muscle and his neck with a bulge beneath it. And to think he's looking better than he ever has. I hate to imagine what I looked like on him before.

'Don't worry about us, we're just fine,' Rose says brightly, speaking for Jupiter too. The stirrups are my length, too short for her, but she doesn't look bothered, only like she's about to go cross country. 'Just ride Ace as if you were in the school, letting her stretch and work through her back.

I promise you, she won't do anything. Any worries, you just tell me, okay?'

'Okay.'

Touching my legs to her side, I squeeze Ace on, asking her to step forward. I expect her to either chuck her head in irritation or plunge forward without letting me have any control, but she does neither, instead moving nicely into a collected walk. The grass is springy under her feet as she moves rhythmically across it, and I do my best to relax, not to think about the devil pony beneath me. I glance at Rose, walking Jupiter beside me, and she smiles encouragingly, not bothered by the tantrum-throwing pony she is astride. Jupi is doing the same things he was with me - chomping the bit, pinning his ears, trying to take off - but with Rose it's less. Whatever she's doing is correcting him, and yet she doesn't even look like she's doing anything at all in the saddle, just sitting there, unfazed.

'How is she?'

'Okay, I think,' I say. Even though my reins are short, there's some slack to them, and yet I can feel Ace's mouth on the other end. Her short mane bobs as she walks, her head carriage still, dark, pointed ears framing my line of vision. My leg is on her without me even thinking about it, squeezing with every stride, in rhythm with Ace's front legs.

We carry on down the bridle path, the track remaining the same as the ground drops. The farther we go, the happier Ace becomes, until I'm not even thinking about her anymore, not even worrying. Jupiter stopped jigging after a few minutes of having Rose on his back, and she now has him walking on a long rein, working his nose to the ground, encouraging him to stretch out his neck. I didn't think it was possible to hack him with the reins at the buckle.

But what interests me, what I realise after twenty minutes, is not that I'm not worried about Ace, but how nice she feels. The neck that felt too narrow now feels athletic and supple. The sensitive character isn't nerve-wracking but exciting because the mare is in tune with my every movement, working with me. And I don't feel like I'm about to be thrown off, just like I'm riding a high level pony.

A rabbit shoots out of an overgrown verge beside us, crossing in front of the ponies' tracks with so much speed that I jump in the saddle, before running off into the distance, its white tail disappearing from sight. Jupiter starts, treating Rose to one of his neck-jarring stops, the kind that shakes you right to the marrow of your bones, but Rose barely moves in the saddle. I brace myself for an explosion from Ace, fear returning, but the mare barely spooks. Almost starts to, only to stop when she sees it's just a rabbit. She then looks at Jupiter as though saying, *Really? All that for a rabbit?* I laugh, and then Rose looks back, at Ace's laid-back attitude, and laughs too.

'See,' Rose says, 'she's not that bad.'

The bridle path twists back to the road, and from the incline we're walking up, before the ground flattens out again, I spot Freya's house in the distance. If I look really hard, I can just make out a chestnut pony in the field beside it, grazing happily. And I don't feel jealousy, don't feel sadness, only excitement. All I've done is walk a pony for half an hour, but for the first time, I feel like I've struck the surface of a treasure chest.

chapter 6

Ace and Jupiter hack almost every day during the weeks that follow. I take Ace the next few times, and then Rose convinces me to try Jupiter again, which is a surprising success. He doesn't tug at the reins, or try to buck and leap. A model pony.

'You've fixed him,' I say, amazed.

'I haven't done anything,' Rose says. 'He was just excited to be out, and now he knows that more hacks are coming, he's happy.'

Both ponies are going brilliantly. They're only walking, with the odd, steady trot, but I couldn't be happier. Riding the ponies across the Suffolk countryside, passing stud driveways and going down bridleways framed by Newmarket hedges. It's not cross country, not competing, not what I thought or hoped I'd be doing this summer, but it's the next best thing.

And even though I can't experience the thrill of competing myself, I can still watch others.

It was bright and sunny early this morning, light flooding my eyes through the curtains before the clocks had even struck five, but it's freezing now. The weather is still clear, blue sky contending with no clouds, but there's a chill in the air, a cold wind that is so strong it feels even colder than it is. I'm wearing shorts, and I'm making up for it by burying myself beneath a coat and scarf.

Rose is trotting Sunny around the warm-up, the brown gelding little perturbed by the wind. Every now and then, when it's blowing directly into his face, he'll jerk his head, like trying to shake away the air current, but it soon passes.

'Sybil!'

I look up from my spot on the grass to see Freya and Nell walking towards me. Nell says something to Freya that I don't catch over the sound of the wind, and detours towards a woman standing farther along the ring, the two falling into a conversation. Freya jogs a few strides to reach me, the wind whipping her ponytail over one shoulder, smiling as she collapses into a sitting position beside me. 'Aren't you freezing?' she says by way of greeting.

I shrug, though the goose bumps on my legs tell a different story. 'I'm fine. How long are you here for?'

'Doesn't matter.' She stretches her long legs out in front of her, tugging at the hems of her knee socks. 'I've already ridden Leo, and Mum's not working, so as long as we want. You?'

'As long as Rose is. I got a ride with her.'

The event, located in the Fens, is close enough that even when I'm not competing, I always come watch, as does Freya. Mum is usually happy enough to drive to local horse trials, but when Rose offered me a lift, Mum was quick to accept on my behalf, claiming she had too much to do at the café as it was without taking a day off.

'Is she riding now?' Freya asks.

I nod. 'She's on Sunny, over there.' I point to the dark horse in the warm-up, currently on a ten-metre circle. 'She rode Paddington in the Intermediate yesterday, too, and he went clear.' I pause as a bay horse canters past, close enough that I can hear him breathing. 'Anyone you want to see?'

'I haven't really looked at the entries that much. Ottiline's riding in the Novice,' she says, referencing yet another rider I know whose parents upgraded her reliable cob to a proven FEI pony. 'Oh, and India's riding soon too. She's got two in the 100, I think.'

'Is that Indiana Humphries?' I ask. Training with the European team coach, Freya has been friendly with a lot of fellow pony competitors for a while. I've been to a few clinics myself, but somehow have never really managed to fall into the same group, never belonged. Freya has. Even on an average pony, she's always managed to establish herself among serious contenders, but it's since she started looking for a new pony some months ago, since the team trainer set Freya up to try Leo and she got an FEI pony of her own, that she's really befriended them. One of these riders is Indiana. I've met her briefly myself, but not exchanged enough words to form an opinion of her. She's thirteen, like Freya and me, but often looks younger and behaves older. At the end of last season, Indiana took on her sister Sophia's rides, two ponies that have been to Europeans before. As if one FEI pony weren't enough, she gets two. One, Fendigo, has been to Europeans multiple times with different riders, while the other, Lakota, achieved all his results with one rider, Alexandra Evans, who is now competing at Advanced level. When Sophia's parents bought them, they were two of - if not *the* - best ponies in England. And while I don't know Sophia any better than I know Indiana, I feel like I know enough to know that I don't want to. She lived up to every privileged rider stereotype there is, known to never look after her own ponies, or take criticism, or accept that she was ever in the wrong. It wasn't long until the ponies' results went downhill, until neither could even get around a course. I've had to piece together information like a jigsaw puzzle, not really seeing the whole picture until everything came together, but Sophia's failure wasn't ever a secret, and a topic of great discussion on the pony circuit, most people finding it humorous and believing in karma. Lakota had only had the one rider before Sophia, and her family claimed that he was a one-person-pony, incorrectly trained by a youngster who hadn't prepared him correctly for someone else. In addition to now riding professionally herself, his past rider, Alexandra, is the daughter of top eventers who have both been around Badminton, so that's hard to believe. I've also heard that Sophia and Indiana's parents very much dislike her, claiming she has been nothing but rude to them since they purchased the pony, and that this is the real reason they try to pin the failures on her back. There's a rumour that she once saw Sophia warming him up in draw reins at an event and waltzed straight up to the combination and sliced the reins with a pair of scissors, but I don't know if that's true or an exaggeration on the Humphrieses' part. The older pony, Fendigo, was the bigger surprise, because she was no stranger to carting around rich kids and was used to doing all the work. Unfortunately for her, there was no way Sophia could blame *this* pony for their failures.

When Sophia aged out of ponies last year, Indiana was

given the rides. Freya said Sophia would have been only too glad to see the back of them, but the many eliminations on their competition cards meant that there was no hope of the parents getting the six figures back they'd spent, and so they stayed. But from what I've seen, Indiana shares none of her sister's qualities, and while it's taking time to get the ponies' confidence back, she is doing a great job with them. And of course since Freya has got Leo, the two have been friendlier than ever. After all, their three ponies were all on a European squad together once upon a time.

'Yeah, but everyone calls her India,' Freya says to me.

'And she's riding Lakota and Fendigo?'

'Otto and Fendi, yeah. I hope she does well,' she adds, sounding like she really means it as she watches the warm-up, and it takes every ounce of self-control I have not to scream, *Why? Why does she deserve to do well, when she's been handed two FEI ponies? If we all got horses that have been on European teams, we'd all be pros by now!* A few months ago, I could have said it out loud, but now that Freya has Leo, I can't.

'How was Leo this morning?' I ask instead.

'Good. I only went for a hack.' A pause as an out of control grey gelding canters past us, so close its feet send sandy dirt flying towards our faces. 'How's Maggot?'

'Ace,' I correct sharply, annoyed. 'Her name's Ace.'

'Sorry, I don't mean it horridly, opposite. It's cute, it suits her.'

'It does not,' I snap. Like I'm ever going to be taken seriously with a pony called Maggot. Not that she's mine, of course. 'But she's fine. Really good, actually. I think I can start jumping her soon.' This last part isn't exactly true, because I haven't even cantered her yet, but Freya doesn't need to know that.

'Good. I like her.' She adds the second sentence as though it has only just occurred to her.

'She's not even in Leo's league,' I say.

Freya almost winces when I say that, the movement visible, but she covers it up. 'They're both just ponies, I'm not saying one's any better than the other. Just saying I like her.' There's another awkward silence, and it occurs to me that Freya hasn't mentioned Jupiter, hasn't asked how he is doing, but I guess he really is beneath her now. Like she and Indiana Humphries and all these other riders whose parents buy them FEI ponies off European teams have time to care about an unsound loan pony that doesn't even go in a correct outline. 'Hey,' Freya says, voice light again, 'there's India.'

I follow her gaze to the lorry park - the *big* lorry park, for those with huge horseboxes, like Rose and the Humphrieses, not the trailer park I'm usually in - and pick India out of the few combinations making their way to the warm-up. She's on Lakota - Otto, Freya called him - a solid light bay with a tiny speck of white on his forehead who is not known for his looks. If you saw him standing in the lorry park, you'd never guess he were capable of what he is. He's naturally chunky, like Jupiter, and nothing about his appearance makes him stand out. Not like Leo, who you'd spot among other chestnuts from a mile away. Otto's a mucker, a get-the-job-done pony, but for all his plainness, he can still put in a very good test.

'Did India ride in the Pony Championships at Brand Hall?' I ask Freya.

'No, of course not. She's not even going around Novice yet.' This time, I know Freya didn't mean for her words to come out harshly, only spoke the facts with the same reserve she does most things. If I didn't know when her briskness is unintentional, we'd have fallen out long ago.

'...and just walk him for a while, India, you've ages till your test,' India's mum says loudly as she walks along the edge of the ring, towards a huddle of people. She's dressed like all wealthy horse mums - slim jeans, designer waistcoat, windswept hair tied back, big sunglasses, walking boots (though this changes to Dubbarys or designer wellies when it's raining) - and her voice is the kind of posh that makes me feel uncomfortable.

'I know, I know, I know,' India says once she's out of her mum's earshot. Her pale blond hair is even thicker and curlier than Freya's, eyes blue and holding a permanently anxious look to them. She's built like Freya, too, all skinny long legs that make dressage tests look good. Otto is on a long rein as they walk this way, and India's face turns to a smile when she spots Freya. 'Hey.'

'Hey,' Freya replies. 'I think you've maybe met Sybil,' she adds as an introduction.

'Hi,' India says kindly, and I say hi back.

'How're you doing?' Freya asks.

'Okay. Breeding season's over, so things are a bit easier. My family breeds Thoroughbreds,' she adds to me.

Of course they do. 'That's really cool.'

India pulls a face. 'Sometimes, but it's a lot of work.'

'They must be cute, though,' I say.

'They get less cute when you have to handle them every day,' India says with a smile. 'You can come by and see them sometime if you want.'

I don't know if she means that, but she seems to, and so far she's much nicer than I expected. 'Thanks, I'd love to someday.'

'Cool. How's Leo?' she asks Freya.

'Good, thanks. We have a lesson with Lydia next week. Is Sophia competing today?' Freya mentioned once that since ageing out of ponies last year, Sophia's parents repeated history by buying her a horse that has been on the *Junior* European team, as if maybe a bigger size will work out better.

'Yesterday,' India replies. 'She came seventh. And then my little sister is riding tomorrow.'

'She's riding affiliated?' Freya asks, surprised. 'I didn't think she was old enough.'

'She's twelve this year, she's just tiny and doesn't look it. Or act it.'

'How are the ponies?'

India nods. 'Okay, thanks.' She looks down at Otto, patting the bay's neck as he stands placidly. 'They both had jumping lessons with Merritt this week and they're doing all right. He's still throwing in the odd stop, though,' she adds, nodding at the pony. 'I need to try and get a chance to talk to Alex later, actually, and ask her something. We're still figuring things out.'

Freya shrugs. 'At least they're improving.'

'Yeah, I guess.' India looks over her shoulder as her mum's voice resonates loudly, laughing at something one of her friends has said. 'I'd better go. See ya around.'

When India has ridden away, far enough not to hear, I turn to Freya. 'Alex is Otto's old rider? I thought that was a World War Three situation?'

'It is with her parents and Sophia,' Freya explains quietly. 'They can't stand each other, but India's not stupid and she knows how well Otto went for her, so a few months ago she started talking to Alex and asking for tips, and Alex now helps her out in secret. India says she's actually really nice, just doesn't always come across that way. Then again, who can blame her for being angry about her one in a million pony being wrecked?'

We watch Rose's round, and stay in the warm-up long enough to see Fendi, India's other pony, be led to the ring by who I can only presume is her little sister. Fendi is much like Otto in that she isn't a looker, but a worker. Does exactly what it says on the tin. She isn't chunkier so much as she's bigger boned, covers more space. She's chestnut, with a flaxen mane and tail, a roman nose along which runs a thick white stripe, and a splash of pink between her nostrils. The little girl leads her around as though she were a dog, so she's obviously easy to do.

I go to help Rose afterwards, holding horses and carrying different spurs and bits in case she changes her mind in the warm-up. Sunny goes double clear with a few time faults to place fourth, which Rose is perfectly happy with. In between her rounds, I get to see some more of India, get to watch her warm up her ponies for show jumping and come out of the ring with faults she did very well to keep in single digits. Both ponies give her a tough time, hesitant on the approach to the fences and then running away on landing, all effects from how they've been ridden these past years. But even when they come out of the ring with bad rounds, and India's mum has a face like thunder, India is calm with them, rewarding them, never showing any sign of being annoyed, and she goes up further in my estimation.

I thought being here would be torture. Watching everyone compete and move forward while I'm on the sidelines, stuck in a never-ending loop of work that doesn't pay off. But it doesn't. Because in a few months' time, Jupiter will be fit and strong and in better shape than he's ever been, ready to tackle the event scene, and Ace - well, Ace isn't mine and will probably be sold, but I might get a chance to compete her this summer, and I'll be able to benefit from the skills I've learned riding a horse so completely different from my own. And who knows, a horse with a nickname like Maggot might not be saleable at all.

chapter 7

'Steady through the turn. Use your outside rein to steady her, not the inside. Good. And more inside leg there.'

Ace rushes away from the contact, throwing me off balance, and I fight the urge to use the inside rein to steady myself. Nothing is going right today. After watching Rose and India compete over the weekend, I was feeling enthusiastic. I was ready to crack on, to get training Ace and Jupiter, training them right, so that I could be out there too. But apparently Ace didn't get the message, because she's not having any of it today.

'I think she might be in season,' Rose says when I bring Ace back to a walk. Despite how great she is on a hack, despite how much happier it seems to make her, she's still uptight in a sand school, and she fidgets anxiously as I try talking to Rose.

'She feels it,' I grumble.

Rose leans back against the railing, crossing her legs, and her arms across her chest. 'Stay in walk and ask her for some shoulder-ins down the long side. Let's try to get her focussed, thinking about something else.'

'Can I still try cantering her today?' I ask. Before the lesson started, Rose, who has been working Ace in canter herself for a few days, told me I could try a few strides to see how I found her, if all went well in the warm-up.

'Depends how well you do all this,' she says again now. 'I want perfect shoulder-ins and half-passes in walk, which we both know she's capable of, and if you can get her going well in trot after that, then you can canter.'

I give the lateral movements my all, first getting Ace onto a ten-metre circle in a corner of the school before carrying on down the long side and using my inside leg to get her moving sideways so that she is walking on three tracks. Eva used to ask me to do lateral movements, but I never really understood what I was doing, and Jupiter wasn't interested enough in dressage to make up for it. I sort of knew the aids for each movement, but I couldn't actually say what the horse was really supposed to do. Rose explained everything to me, how the horse is supposed to move and how to correct easy mistakes, but to top it off, as Rose said, Ace already knows the movements. At some point in her early schooling she clearly had somebody on her back who knew what they were doing, because she responds to the lightest touch, will start crossing her legs as soon as you come down the centre line on the right rein and start pushing her with the left leg. And for the first time I felt what the movements are actually supposed to feel like, her quarters moving beneath me, being in control of every footfall.

'Good,' Rose tells me as I rejoin the track after a perfect half-pass. 'All right, get her working the same in trot and you can try a few strides of canter.'

Be it because she's in season or just because she is what she is, Ace really isn't in the best mood today. She's feisty in trot, going forward in an outline but not actually staying between my hand and leg. She isn't as cold-backed as she was before, but you still never feel like you're really safe in the saddle, unlike Jupiter who feels like glue most of the time. I'm used to it now, having to balance myself because there's no way the mare will help, but she is worse today. Considering how much better than this she's been going, even I know it probably isn't the day to attempt a canter, especially when Rose has already explained to me how you have to be very quiet in your seat and not catch her in the mouth or she'll run off, but I'm so bored of waiting.

Ace executes the same lateral movements in trot, albeit with less style, and despite feeling irritated, she does whatever I ask.

'Can I try a canter?' I ask Rose again, trotting Ace on a twenty-metre circle as I speak.

Rose hesitates, and I know full well what she's thinking, the same thing I am, really, but am trying to ignore. 'Are you sure? She doesn't look as settled as she has,' she says cautiously.

'I think I can manage,' I tell her, trying to sound as confident as I can. 'If it doesn't go well, I'll stop.'

She still doesn't look convinced. 'Just a few strides, then back to trot. Ride really soft, because she does tense up in the transition.'

'I will,' I say.

My heart thuds hard in my chest as I collect Ace again, getting ready to ask for a canter. I circle her once more, making sure I have some sort of balance and control, and when I get to the corner of the school, I stick my outside leg behind the girth and sit deep in the saddle.

If I were on Jupiter, he would have popped lazily into a canter, moving on while I found a sitting rhythm. But Ace is not Jupiter, and the forceful aid sends her shooting forward - in a canter, granted - and I barely have time to gather my reins before she launches into a series of bucks, taking off around the school. I hear Rose's voice urgently telling me to sit up, but I can't focus on anything other than trying not to fall. I pull desperately at the reins, but that only makes Ace worse, and she rushes away further.

I lose count of how many laps of the school we do, only know that the mare does eventually fall back to a trot before I can fall off, which I know would have happened if she hadn't, head high and nostrils flared. My whole body is shaking from the fear and the effort, and I bring her back to a walk as quickly as I can, fighting back tears. I should've listened. I knew she wasn't in the right frame of mind to try something new today.

'Are you okay?' Rose asks, laying one hand on my leg and the other on Ace's neck.

I nod, knowing any words will make the tears I'm fighting to hold back fall freely.

'You did well to stay on.' A pause. 'Do you know what you did wrong?'

Of course, the *I told you so* speech. I shrug, not knowing what to say.

Rose goes on. 'You were too forceful in your aids. It's not your fault, because you've always had to ride like that. Jupiter wouldn't have thought anything of it, because he's dead to the leg. But Ace doesn't need that kind of force. She needs to be eased into things, because she runs away when she's afraid. You surprised her by sticking your leg on like that, so her first instinct was to flee. But you did so well to stay on.'

'I'm so stupid,' I mutter, wiping my eyes.

'No, you're not. You're young and you're learning on a difficult pony far beyond your level. The only way you learn is by making mistakes. Most people your age are going around on five-figure schoolmasters, am I right?'

Yes, they are. Freya with perfect Leo, and Indiana with not one but two incredible ponies I doubt she has to look after herself. I nod.

'You don't have to ride her, you know,' Rose says. 'I only thought you might like having something to work, but nobody's making you.'

Maybe I shouldn't. Maybe I should just stop riding Ace and continue working Jupiter and then he'll be ready to compete again in no time. He's started trotting and cantering now, under Rose's watchful eye, and is feeling fitter than he's ever felt before. And yet... 'I *do* want to ride her,' I say, flicking a stray strand of mane over to the right side. 'I just wish I wasn't so useless.'

'You're not useless. You're inexperienced on an inexperienced pony.' She strokes Ace's neck, which is damp with sweat. 'Now, are you going to try again?'

With Rose coaching me, I manage to get Ace to canter again without taking off in a leaping bucking fit. She still rushes, still doesn't really stay between my hand and leg, and any attempt to take a check on a rein is met with head tossing, but it's a canter none the less. Her gait isn't actually uncomfortable to sit so much as it's stressful, because like in trot, you feel like she could decide to throw you onto the ground at any moment.

'This is what she's always done,' Rose tells me after the

lesson, when I've dismounted and am leading Ace back to the yard. 'She started running away with Beatrix when she was riding her. They had her back and teeth and everything checked, of course, made sure the problem was nothing physical, and as it wasn't, they just kept going. They pushed and over-faced her, and that made things worse.'

'But why did she start doing it?'

'Who knows. Beatrix isn't the best rider, so the mare probably just started losing her confidence, and was never helped to regain it. She's naturally anxious anyway, and then things were just made worse. She got quicker and quicker to jump, and their solution was just to whack the fences up so she had to slow down.' Rose shakes her head. 'Ridiculous. It's one of my biggest pet peeves. Putting fences up to get a horse to be more careful and use his head is one thing, but something that's young and running away? A joke. If you can't get a horse safely over fifty centimetres, then you shouldn't be jumping any higher.'

'That makes sense, I guess.' The barn cats run past Ace as we walk across the concrete, the two tabbies pursuing a mouse, and she follows them with her eyes. 'So what do we do? How do we fix the problem?'

Rose taps her head with her index finger. 'You've got to fix this. You've got to earn her trust and get her to listen to you, so that when she gets scared, her first instinct isn't to run away.'

'She doesn't on a hack,' I point out.

'No, she doesn't, and we need the same thing in a school. Her first instinct when she's scared is to run away, and her second instinct needs to be to run to you, until staying there becomes the only thing she does when she's unsure. Before trying to earn her trust in the saddle, I think you need to earn her trust on the ground. Get her to follow you in the school. Walk when you walk, stop when you stop. Over poles and between fillers. Really get her to trust you. Get her to respond to the sound of your voice, so that if she does take off, you have a way of getting through to her. And you know what? I'd even try schooling her bareback.'

'Bareback?' I have a hard enough time staying on with a saddle.

'I really think it could help. She's calm on a hack because she doesn't associate it with work and bad memories, and bareback could be the same. She needs to have fun and learn to be a horse again. And you need to work her without me hovering about, so the two of you find your way.'

I'm not convinced, but I mumble some sort of agreement as I lead Ace back to her stable. My legs are killing me from trying to stay on when she took off earlier, aching with every step. I untack her quickly, feeling more positive than I did some moments ago, and as I fish a dandy brush out of her grooming box, mind elsewhere as I let myself back into the stable, I'm met by a sharp pinch, a throbbing pain, to my arm.

'Ouch!'

Ace jumps back, pinning her ears, and lets out a lazy snort, as though *I* have offended her by not being happy she just bit me.

'Seriously?' I say, arm still stinging. I'm sure it will be purple by tomorrow. 'You know what? You really are a Maggot.'

I'm not convinced it's going to help at all, but I start doing groundwork with Ace. It all seems a bit ridiculous to me, like the rope twirling in this TV series about a horse whisperer that Freya is obsessed with, but I do it. And the funny thing is, in no time at all, not only do I see what she lacks, but how little attention I've paid to these little details.

When I walk Ace, only in a head collar as I stand at her shoulder, she doesn't stay beside me. She's well-mannered to turn out and bring in from the paddock, but not walking around the school like this. She tries to pull ahead, or walk into me, or not move at all. It's like trying to teach the dogs to walk on leads, getting them to heel and not just drag you off into the distance as Frodo does. I have to get Ace to actually listen to me, pay attention to me, not just do her own thing. And it doesn't take very long. After one session, she walks when I walk, stops when I stop, backs up when I take a step backwards. It's so easy, and yet she didn't do it before, and I realise how often we get on horses we haven't mastered on the ground, and wonder how much trouble could be saved just by taking the time to do these little exercises.

I keep going, day after day. After walking, I run, getting Ace to trot alongside me. Then we incorporate transitions and poles, until she's in tune with my every movement. And then, when she's mastered that, I do it without the rope. I unclip it from her head collar but keep it in my hand, and repeat the exercises. Ace walks beside me, turning when I turn, stops when I stop. When I click my tongue and break into a run, she trots with me, and when I come back to a walk, she does, too. I use my voice whenever I make a transition, remembering Rose's advice that I get the mare used to voice commands. At first it's simple - *whoa* means stop and a cluck means go - but then I make it more complicated. I start saying *walk* when I mean walk, *trot* when

I mean trot, *canter* when I mean canter, *halt* when I want her to stop, stretching out the word, and I save *whoa* for when I just need her to slow down. I wouldn't have thought it possible, certainly not with Ace, but she differentiates between them all, until my voice is the only thing I need to control her. Even without me beside her, she does whatever I ask, and it isn't long until I am standing in the middle of the school with her on circle around me, lunging without a rope. And she doesn't just rush about with her head in the air, either, but drops her nose to the sand, stretching through her back, working her body without the help of any accessories.

'It's like magic!' Rose says one day, grinning from ear to ear as she watches from the railings. Ace is trotting on a circle around me, and when I ask her to come back to walk, she does, and I tell her to halt before walking up to her, showering her with praise. She may be listening to me now, but she still doesn't exactly show me anything that resembles affection, pinning her ears and doing her best to look aggressive when I give her attention.

'I can't believe it,' I say, clipping the rope back to the head collar. 'I've never worked a horse on the ground before. Do you really think it will help her under saddle?'

Rose nods. 'I do.'

I grin, scratching Ace's neck, and she lifts a hind leg in protest. A few weeks ago, this would have bothered me, but now I know it's just how she is. 'I'll have to try with Jupi, too,' I say. 'He never stops next to me when I try to stop him.'

'She is particularly good at it, though,' Rose says, inclining her head towards Ace. '*Because* she's so uptight and anxious. She actually wants to have a relationship with you, wants to connect and trust you, and she's so sharp. That's the problem too, really. She's too bright for her own good.'

'So, what next?'

Rose fixes her eyes on me, as though waiting for me to go on. I know what she wants me to say.

'Bareback?'

'Yep. I really think you'll be amazed.'

I look at the funny mare, and - I notice for the first time - her particularly prominent withers. 'If you say so.'

'And maybe in a head collar, too. So she doesn't fuss.'

'Do you just want to see me fall off?'

Rose laughs. 'Course not. Then I'd be stuck doing her on my own. But you've got control of her now, so you shouldn't need anything other than your voice.'

If I was unsure about groundwork, I'm even more dubious about riding an event horse bareback, let alone one like Ace, but I can't say that the former hasn't been a success, so I give it a go.

I thought I felt unsafe in a saddle, but that seems like a seatbelt compared to this.

'Don't clench your legs,' Rose says. 'You know she doesn't like that.'

'But if I don't, I have no balance,' I argue as Ace takes a few tentative steps beneath me. 'If she took off, I'd be on the floor.'

'Well you're just going to have to trust her not to, aren't you?'

I wouldn't say that I trust Ace, nowhere near, but after a few minutes of walking, during which she doesn't try to throw me off, I begin to relax, if for no other reason than boredom. But she's calmer than she ever has been under saddle in the school, more like how she is on a hack. Soon my worries ease away, and when I ask her to trot, only by speaking the command, she bounces into the pace, which is much more comfortable than I anticipated, and moves with balance and lift, carrying herself in an outline.

'Not too much wrong with that now, is there?' Rose calls.

I grin, lost in Ace's rhythm. We circle and serpentine and come back to walk and then trot again, her attitude never changing. Never did I think I could like this mare as much as I do now.

After some time, when I'm so relaxed on Ace's back that I've completely stopped grabbing mane or clenching my legs whenever I get nervous, I ask her to canter. Don't touch my legs to her sides, don't drive her with my seat, just say the word, knowing full well that she could decide to take off and buck, but it doesn't matter. I want her to trust me, so I have to trust her. Give and take.

The mare moves forward fluidly, no hesitation, no rush, and falls into a canter, her neck arched as she carries her head perpendicular to the ground. I don't lose my balance, don't feel like I'm going to fall, just go with her.

'You look happy.'

I fall onto one of the chairs, resting my elbows on the table. 'I am. Ace was amazing.'

'I'm glad,' Mum says, smiling at me. She looks back down at the papers in front of her and sighs before gathering them neatly into a pile. 'You know, I think I've had enough work for today.' She glances at the sofa on which Gabe is reading, lying on his back, both dogs asleep on the other one, then looks back at me. 'I'd better find something for dinner.'

'What are you reading?' I ask Gabe.

'Something from the phone box,' he says. 'It's amazing,' he adds briskly, never taking his eyes off the page, so I say nothing further, because he's clearly enthralled.

Mum is in the kitchen, looking through the fridge and opening cupboards, and I drag her papers across the table, frowning as I try to make sense of the accounts. Just looking at the pages makes my head hurt, and that's without even having to understand them. I look at Mum again, her face lit up by the refrigerator light, and notice the dark circles around her eyes, the creases in her forehead. Whenever I go to Home Stretch it's packed, and I can't imagine having to be responsible for the business.

'Okay, so we have no food.' Mum closes the fridge door, tucking a wisp of hair behind her ear as she regards me and Gabe. 'I'll go pick up pizzas if one you orders them online.'

'I'll do it,' I say, opening her laptop.

She sits back down, yawning as she stretches her arms overhead, cradling the back of her head in her hands. 'So Ace was good?'

'Really, really good. I cantered her bareback, and she was amazing. And I rode Jupi before her and he feels the best he's ever felt. Rose helped me on the flat, and she says he looks amazing. And you know how he always used to get lazy halfway through a lesson? Well, he doesn't do that anymore. And I know he'd never sweat, but he used to blow a lot, and he doesn't do that now, either.'

Mum smiles. 'I'm glad. I'm so glad. Thank you,' she says suddenly. 'Both of you. I know this hasn't been easy, moving here and everything, and I know I'm working a lot, but… thank you, that's it. I'm very lucky to have you two.'

Gabe shrugs without looking away from his book. 'I like

it here.'

'Yeah,' I say. 'Me too.'

Mum smiles again. 'Me too.'

'And sorry to change the subject,' I say to Mum, 'but can I ask you something?'

'You just did,' Gabe calls.

I ignore him. 'Do I still have my back account?'

Mum frowns dubiously. 'Hmm, which bank account would that be?'

I glare at her, and humour the question with a response. 'The one you put my dad's' - *my dad*, as in my biological father, not Dad - 'child support payments into. Well, what's left over each month.' What's left over is often very little, but I know that Mum has always made a point of putting some aside, ever since I was little. *For uni or a rainy day,* in her words. And if Ace isn't a tornado then I don't know what is.

'Of course. I'd never touch that.' Her face slowly breaks into a grin. 'Dare I ask why?'

I grin back. 'Probably best you don't.'

chapter 8

The joyous mood is short-lived.

Ace continues to improve, and when I start riding her under saddle again, which is still a grey area, I find that all the work we've done is paying off. She's more anxious, and can throw in the odd buck and spook, but I'm able to control her more easily, and she listens to my voice. At the start of summer, I never thought she'd become as quiet as this in such a short time. But while the improvement is immense, I still can't see her being ready to sell on anytime soon.

When Rose mentions an unaffiliated dressage outing, one she's taking her event horses to, and suggests that Ace and I tag along, I'm thrilled. But when I hurry home to tell Mum, she bursts my bubble.

'You can't go to a competition tomorrow, Sybs.'

'What? Why not? It's not like it's a real competition, anyway.'

'I don't care what it is, it's not possible.' She puts her hands on her hips and stares me straight in the eye. 'Have you forgotten? What day is it today?'

'Um, Friday? What has that got to do with anything?'

Mum pulls a face, the typical "I'm so disappointed in you" face. 'Sybil, you know your dad's picking you and Gabe up tonight.'

'That's tonight?'

'Yes, and he should be here any minute so go get ready.'

'Do I have to go?' I sigh. 'Can't I just not go this time and ride Ace tomorrow?'

'No, you cannot,' Mum says firmly. 'Every other weekend, you're at your dad's. End of. I'll look after Jupi, and you go and spend time with your dad.'

'He isn't even my dad,' I snap, then instantly feel bad.

Mum holds a finger up, disappointment fading and anger taking its place. 'Don't even go there. You know he'd never say the same about you.'

'But, Mum, please,' I say, moving on. 'This is the first time Rose has said I can take Ace somewhere. And I already told her yes, I can't let her down.'

'I'll explain to Rose that you forgot about going to your dad's, and I guarantee she'll be on my side over this. The answer is no, Sybil, and I don't want to keep discussing this.'

'I don't like London. It's not safe.'

'Riding horses isn't safe,' Mum says.

'But it's not like I'm going to have that many more chances to ride Ace. She'll be sold soon.'

'Last I heard, you were planning on doing something about that, and if you still want me to even consider it, then I suggest you get upstairs now and pack a suitcase.'

Eventually I realise I'm beat, and I throw some clothes and books into a bag with little enthusiasm, unsure which parent I'm angriest with. Both of them, for making things be like this. It's like they need special attention now that they're no longer together. Before, it wouldn't have mattered if Gabe or I chose to do something ourselves above spending time with one of our parents, but now that's not an option.

But then Dad arrives, and he's jolly as always, hugging us and talking about how excited he is and asking what we want for dinner, and I feel even worse about what I said and thought earlier.

'That's a nice house, isn't it?' Dad says when we're in the car - me in the passenger seat, Gabe in the back - nodding at Liam's place.

'Yeah, but the guy who lives there is weird,' Gabe says.

'Is he?'

'Yeah. He never leaves the house, he barely speaks, and he has this white cat that follows him everywhere. We think he's a vampire, don't we, Sybil?'

'We don't know anything about him,' I snap. Truth is, Gabe and I *have* said that, and worse, and Liam *is* weird, from what I've seen of him, anyway, but we also don't know what his life is like. Recently, I've found that everything and everyone I thought I knew has turned out differently from what I expected, nothing proving as it seems, and I wonder if Liam's the same.

I'm leaning on the fence post, watching Jupiter and Ace graze with Cinder and Pheasant, when a chirpy voice I know all too well cuts into my thought.

'Sybil! What're you doing? Are you riding?' Mackenzie bounds up beside me, all toothy smile and flying plaits. She and Jemima recently returned from a week with their grandparents, Ben's parents, and the yard was noticeably quieter.

'I will be,' I say. 'I'm riding Ace with your mum later and I need to work Jupiter now, but I was just watching them.' I pause, staring at the happy ponies, the late afternoon sun shining down on them, Ace the biggest and the brightest, but all four the picture of health. Ace is with Cinder, her confidante, the two grazing side by side, while Pheasant is farther away, and Jupiter is nearest. He hasn't even looked up, too content pulling at the blades of grass, tail swishing at the occasional fly, and the sight of him just makes me so happy. I always worried that he didn't get to go out in the field much, long before meeting Rose, but now that he does, now that he never goes a day without spending hours in the grass, free to roam as he wishes, with other horses, and sometimes spends the whole night out, it makes me sick. To think he used to be out the same amount of time in two months what he now is in one day. No wonder his body wasn't working properly. How could he *not* be stiff, confined to a box his whole life?

'Can I ride with you?' Mackenzie asks, both eager and cautious.

'Uh, yeah, sure. I mean, it's your school, anyway,' I point out.

'No, it's never our school,' Mackenzie says seriously. 'It's boarders' school, and we mustn't act like it's ours.'

I smile at her words, able to believe exactly how Rose must have said the same things to her and Jemima multiple times. 'All right. Let's ride.'

Forty minutes later, I'm doubled over with laughter over Jupiter's neck.

'See,' Mackenzie says, 'I told you I could ride standing up.'

Cinder is bareback - her rider ditched the saddle ages ago - while Mackenzie stands on top of her, holding the reins as the bay mare walks around the school. When she told me, while I was schooling Jupiter, that she could ride standing up, I didn't disagree or say I didn't believe her so much as I didn't really say anything, which she immediately interpreted as a challenge. And I'm forced to admit that Mackenzie is right - she *can* ride standing up.

'I can trot too,' Mackenzie says. 'Trot on, Cinder.' She clucks at her. 'Go on.'

The ageing mare moves dozily into a trot, going in an outline even under these circumstances, and Mackenzie remains balanced on top. Cinder trots half a circle before veering off to the right, causing her rider to wobble, and Mackenzie lets out a small cry as she lets her feet slide, landing on her pony's back, and she bursts out laughing as she almost falls, grabbing a handful of mane to right herself.

'Wahoo, didn't fall,' Mackenzie cries, throwing an arm up triumphantly.

I laugh further, Jupiter resting a leg with boredom.

Mackenzie brings Cinder to a halt. 'Wanna go?'

I shake my head. 'Nah, I don't think I can do that. And if I fall, I won't be able to help your mum with Ace.'

'You can still ride her. Do you want to? She's really good, I promise.'

'That's okay-'

'No, really, go on.' Mackenzie swings off the mare, making it clear that she isn't taking no for an answer. 'I'll hold Jupiter for you.'

'Well, you can ride him,' I say.

Mackenzie looks shocked. 'I couldn't ride your pony.'

'Of course you can. You're asking me to ride yours.'

'But you're a livery. Liveries never ask me to ride their ponies.'

I'm not sure what to respond to that, so I go on. 'Really, he's good. So long as your mum won't mind,' I add, unsure how Rose feels about her children riding other ponies, though knowing her I can't imagine she'll mind. She's around, anyway.

'Okay,' Mackenzie says. She walks up to Jupiter, letting go of Cinder without any worry of the mare walking off. 'Hello Jup. I love him,' she tells me seriously, grinning shyly as her fingers trail down his forelock. 'I always say hello to him when I pass his stable. He's so lovely.'

'He is,' I agree. Even though Jupiter's been on a strict exercise and rehab program since I've been here, he's still bombproof in a school, and a kid like Mackenzie could hardly cause him much damage, and I regret not offering before, if she really is so fond of him. The first thing she did upon meeting me was offer up her pony, after all. 'Should I hold Cinder?' I ask, glancing at the mare as she stands on her own.

'No, she won't move.'

'Okay. Let me shorten your stirrups and I'll help you up, then.'

Staying on the ground long enough to make sure that Mackenzie is okay, I watch Jupiter walk around the school, his rider sitting lightly in the saddle, face determined. Mackenzie is a good little rider, and for all her usual confidence, she's very reserved when she gets on my pony, asking me how he likes to be ridden and making sure she doesn't overstep.

'You need to ride, too,' she tells me. 'You can do anything with her, she'll love it.'

She might not be very big, but I can't get on Cinder from the ground - even though I've been practising with Ace - and I use a filler to get on, settling on her bare back. She's broader than Ace, withers less prominent, and I quickly feel at ease. She's not as dead to the leg as Jupiter, having never been badly schooled, but she isn't as responsive as Ace, either.

'Look at this!' Rose calls, smiling widely as she approaches the school from the house. As I expected, there is no hint of worry or anger in her voice.

'I hope it's okay I said she could ride him,' I say quickly.

'Of course it's okay! I hope it's okay with *you.*'

'Of course. Mackenzie wanted me to try Cinder, so it was only fair.'

'Mum, look, I'm riding Jupiter!' Mackenzie calls.

'That you are. I hope you've thanked Sybil. That's very nice of her.'

'I will, I will,' Mackenzie assures her, before launching into thanks and offering to bake me a cake of my choosing.

'Thank you for letting me ride Cinder,' I say. 'Do you want to try trotting him?'

Mackenzie is hesitant, clearly worried about taking charge of my pony, but I assure her I don't mind, and with Rose's encouragement she pushes Jupiter into a trot. As nice as it is to see how good my pony's looking, how he's developing muscle in all the right places and gleaming with good health, it's even nicer to see how happy he's making Mackenzie. And she's more effective than she looks, too, getting the pony into a nice shape and rhythm with little visible effort. When Mackenzie brings Jupiter back to a walk, she's grinning from ear to ear, dimples in her cheeks.

'He's so so good.' She leans forward to wrap her arms

around his neck. 'Thank you so much.'

'You rode him really well,' I tell her honestly. 'And thank you for Cinder,' I add, swinging off the mare's back.

'Good ponies,' Rose says, standing between them to rub both of their necks. 'Thank you,' she mouths to me when Mackenzie's back is turned, too busy fussing over Jupiter, and I smile at her before looking away, feeling awkward.

'Thank you,' Mackenzie says to me again, and she wraps her arms around me this time, hugging me tightly a moment before letting go and returning to the ponies. I make an effort to look anywhere else, feeling my eyes swim again. Doing something nice for someone has a way of making you feel worse for all you haven't done before. Especially when it's something as simple as this.

'Well,' Rose says, 'as much as I'd love to keep hanging out with these two, there's one more pony that might not be so amusing.'

Ace rushes away from my leg, trying to evade the contact, but I steady her with my voice and my seat, keeping my leg on, and eventually she settles, coming into the hand.

'Good,' Rose says. 'Really good. Bring her back to trot again then ask for another transition.'

I drop my weight further to my heels, sitting tall, and close my fingers on the reins, holding the outside one more firmly. Ace falls into a trot, trying to duck her nose, but I keep her moving forward, pace collected, and then ask for another transition. She swings into canter with a swish of her tail, and I encourage her on, falling into a rhythm.

'And come back to trot when you're ready and walk.'

I give Ace her head when she's back in walk, allowing her to stretch her nose to the ground, and look at Rose, who is adjusting a cross pole. 'Good,' she says again. 'Really good. Just keep riding her like that. Okay, get her back into a nice trot, however long that takes, and when you're ready, turn her to the cross. The placing pole is there so you don't have to think about the stride. Just think of keeping her straight and balanced, a strong trot. Approach it no differently from the poles we just did. Okay?'

'Okay.' We've already spent half an hour warming up, working Ace over trotting poles, both in a straight line and fanned out so that she goes over them on a circle, and while she was good, she was fizzier than she has been recently. Rose has already jumped her this week, already explained to me the main dos and don'ts, and all that's left for me to do is try it myself.

Keeping an eye on the jump, I get Ace back into a trot, circling near the fence so that she has time to see it, take in the new pole layout. Once I feel like she's in a good rhythm, I seek the jump out with my eyes again and start turning towards it. Already through the turn, the mare isn't paying attention. She's tilting her head, intentionally looking anywhere but the fence, and when she does finally see it, she baulks, planting her front feet.

'Yeah, she told you she was going to do that before you'd even turned,' Rose tells me. 'When she sends you a postcard like that you have to correct it, not just wait for her to misbehave. She's sensitive, but you still have to ride her. And again.'

I circle Ace again, beginning to feel discouraged, and once she's moving with impulsion, between my hand and leg, I turn her back to the fence. She starts to slow down again, eyes out on stalks as though this fence were something she's never seen before, but I keep going, building momentum, and as we reach the placing pole, for a moment, I think she's going to stop.

My hesitation doesn't go unnoticed, and Ace slows right down, almost to a standstill, only to launch herself into the air, cat leaping the fence, throwing me back into the seat of the saddle with a thump, and just as I start to regain my balance on landing, she blows. Ace squeals, bolting like she's never bolted with me before, leaping and bucking and galloping all at once. Rose calls out panicked words of advice, but my brain has switched off, paralysed by fear as I fight to stay on, leaning back with my feet out in front of me, desperately trying to regain my reins. But Ace knows what she's doing, isn't playing around, and as she gallops a lap of the school, her ears lock on to the fence, the same fence, and she flies forward, taking off into the air to jump the obstacle, taking the placing pole as a fence with it, and the only positive is that I mange to cling on just long enough for her to be clear of the poles before falling to the sand.

'Hey, how did your lesson go?'

I storm past Mum, who is seated at the table, face scrunched as I refuse to meet her eyes. Food, I need food. And water.

'Sybil?' Mum says. 'Did something go wrong?'

'I don't want to talk about it,' I snap, tears audible in my voice. I pull a glass from the cupboard and pour myself some Ribena, my vision blurred.

'What happened?' Mum looks at me, and I know she's taking in the sand on my jodhpurs, a telltale sign I've eaten dirt. 'Did you fall?'

'What does it look like?' I snap, filling my glass with

water, watching it mix with the cordial and turn pink. I swallow a mouthful before slamming the glass down on the counter.

'Hey, come on, tell me what happened.'

'What happened is I'm stupid and useless and can't ride and never will.'

'Sybil-'

'It's true,' I scream, tears and anger taking control of my face and rendering me incomprehensible. 'Every time things are starting to go well, I do something wrong and mess everything up. Everyone else knows how to ride but me. I just can't do anything right and I ruin ponies and I shouldn't even bother riding because I'm just useless.'

'Sybil-'

'Stop saying my name,' I yell. 'You're not helping. All you do is say my name again and again whenever something goes wrong because you just never know what to do! Everyone else's parents buy them European ponies while I'm stuck trying to ride other people's rejects and I'm just wasting my time because I'll never be as good as them.'

'I understand you've had a bad time,' Mum says tensely, her voice losing some of the sympathy it had a moment ago, 'and I know you're upset, but don't for one moment tell me that owning a hundred-thousand-pound pony is normal, and don't you dare for one moment pity yourself. Hard things happen, and I know life doesn't always seem fair, especially not at the moment, but do not feel sorry for yourself about the ponies you have because most people in the world would kill to have a pony at all. You can be angry and you can be upset and you can acknowledge that some of your friends may have it easier than you, but do not think for one moment that you are unfortunate.'

I want to scream. I want to yell that they're not even my ponies, that what she's saying doesn't change the fact that I have to watch people around me live lives I could only dream of, but instead I break down, and Mum walks across the room to wrap her arms around me, and I cry into her shoulder, too hysterical to form words.

'Now,' she says after a while, after I've stopped hiccuping, 'why don't you calmly tell me what happened.'

The words come tumbling out, about how I first made Ace refuse and then almost made her refuse again but she still managed to jump despite me, and how she took off and I fell. Tears fall again as I tell the story, body shaking, and I wish I could go back to an hour ago, when I was laughing with Mackenzie and feeling on top of the world.

'Are you hurt?'

I shake my head. I may have a bruise tomorrow, but nothing more.

'And did you not get back on.'

'No, I did.' I wipe my cheeks with my sleeve. 'Rose got on first and took Ace over the cross, and of course she was fine with her, and then I got on and did it again. But it was still all my fault.'

'But you got back on,' Mum says. 'That's all that matters. You can make every mistake in the book, and you can fall a hundred times, but it doesn't mean anything if you get back on. *That* is all that matters. Do you want to keep riding Ace?'

'Yes. I don't know. I want to be good enough to ride her.'

'And you will be, if you keep going. If you want to give up then say the word, because nobody is making you do this, but the only way you'll get past this is if you stick with it.'

I've just about stopped crying when Gabe comes back in from walking the dogs. Frodo runs up to me when he's let off his lead, tail wagging, and I bury my face in his thick neck. There's nothing a dog hug can't solve.

'Have you seen what's happened to Liam?' my brother says, not noticing, much to my relief, my tear-stained face.

'No.' Mum sits up straighter. 'What's happened?'

'I haven't seen him in a while but he was putting the bins out. Anyway, he's broken his leg.'

'What?'

Gabe nods enthusiastically, as though it were a happy occurrence. 'He's got a cast on and is walking on crutches.'

'How could he injure himself?' I say. 'I've never seen him leave the house.'

'Well, he has.'

'Why didn't he come here?' Mum says, surprising both Gabe and me with her naive tone. 'I specifically told him that that's what we're here for. Did I not say the words broken limb?'

'That's probably what happened,' Gabe says. 'You cursed him.'

'Oh, don't be ridiculous.'

'He probably has family to do that,' I point out to Mum.

She shakes her head. 'He lives there alone, I'm certain. I've never seen anyone else there.'

'Maybe he doesn't like us,' Gabe ventures.

'Oh, we've got to do something for him.' Mum jumps up, heading for the kitchen, and pulls a box out of the fridge. 'Perfect, I brought a cheesecake home from the café for us for dessert.'

'Hey, that's my favourite.' Gabe stares sadly at the box. 'Do we really have to give him that? Can't we give him something else? He might not even like cheesecake.'

'Then he can feed it to the cat for all I care, but we're offering it to him. Go on, take it round now.'

'Now?' I repeat.

'Yes. For all we know his leg's been broken a week and he hasn't eaten in that time.'

'But he's weird,' Gabe says.

'So are all of us. Now go.'

And that's how we find ourselves standing at Liam's front door, like the beginning of a horror moving, waiting for somebody in the creepy-looking house to answer.

'We're probably about to be murdered,' Gabe whispers to me.

'Shh. Someone's coming.'

The sound of what I know are crutches echoes on the other side of the door, followed by turning locks and sliding bolts. Liam's head appears around the side of the door, looking much like he normally does. Too pale to have ever spent more than a minute in the sun, hair tousled, brown eyes behind a pair of rectangular glasses.

'Hello,' he says slowly.

'We brought cheesecake,' says Gabe.

'We heard you'd been injured,' I explain, shooting my brother a look, 'and so our mum wanted to bring you something. She owns a café,' I add, as though that should explain why we have spare cheesecakes lying around.

'Okay.' He looks down at the box, and I notice that he's wearing the same thing he was when I first met him. I hope the clothes have been washed since then. 'Thank you.'

Gabe holds the box out to Liam, who reaches to take it, but the crutches fall from his arms, and he's left fighting to keep his balance. I hit Gabe in the arm for being so stupid and bend to retrieve Liam's crutches, handing them back to him. 'Give me that,' I snap at Gabe, taking the box. I look at Liam again. 'Do you want me to carry it in for you?'

He looks over his shoulder, making no attempt to hide his deliberation, and then back at us, as though this pains him. 'Sure, I guess you could do that. The place is a bit of a mess, though.'

'That's okay,' I say.

'You should see ours,' Gabe adds.

Liam doesn't smile, but his expression softens, and he steps aside, holding the door ajar to let us in. I urge Gabe on first, preparing myself to walk into one of those filthy houses you see on TV. Mum watched a show once about wealthy people in stately homes who never cleaned or threw a single belonging away, and the places were overflowing with rubbish and dirt, which is what I'm expecting this to be. But the hallway isn't, to my relief. Immaculate, if anything. Wood-panelled walls adorned with antique mirrors and paintings, waxed floors, a few pieces of mahogany furniture. Like a room I'd expect to read about in a fantasy book about an orphan being swept off to live with a relative in some deserted manor.

'Uh, the kitchen's over here,' Liam says.

We follow him through a doorway, into a kitchen much smaller than you'd expect for a house this size, and I almost drop the cheesecake when the white cat jumps off one of the kitchen cabinets, landing onto the table with a thud.

'Off you get,' Liam tells it, pushing the ball of fluff aside, and I put the box down lest the creature should attempt any more death-defying jumps.

'She's sweet,' Gabe says, either not seeing or not caring that Liam doesn't particularly seem to want us here, making himself at home as he starts stroking the cat. 'Is it a she?'

'Um, yes,' Liam says, meeting my eyes briefly, as though thinking the same thing I am.

Gabe goes on stroking her, fingers finding the tag around her collar. 'Amity Byron,' he reads. 'That's her name?'

'Yes,' Liam says briskly. But Gabe isn't finished.

'Like the character in *The Quest of Byron*?'

An emotion flickers across Liam's face, something different from what I've seen from him so far, but I can't tell what it is. 'You know *The Quest of Byron*?'

Gabe nods enthusiastically. 'I've read all three books and I'm waiting for the fourth. It's so good. You've read it? Your cat's named after the character? Hey, there's a white cat in that too, isn't there? But it's obviously not called Amity Byron, because that's the main character. It's called-'

'Leopold,' Liam finishes.

'Yes, Leopold. And obviously you couldn't have called her Leopold, because she's a girl.'

'Right.'

Silence falls across the room, and I nudge Gabe's arm. 'Hey, we should probably let Liam get back to-'

'You like those books?' Liam goes on, cutting me off. I'm too surprised to hear him speak voluntarily to say anything.

'They're my new favourites. Sybil's reading the first one, too.'

'I've only just started it,' I say.

'What do you think's going to happen in the fourth?' Gabe asks Liam. 'I think that Amity going off with Cassius, accepting his help to avenge her father's death-'

'Hey,' I interrupt, covering my ears. 'Spoiler!'

'-is a trick. I think she's bluffing, I don't think she really trusts him.'

Liam smiles, the first I've seen from him. 'Is that so?'

Gabe nods. 'Yep.'

'Come on, Gabe,' I say again, grabbing on to his arm. 'We need to leave.'

I manage to get him to the hallway, the room that is like something out of a castle, before his attention is caught by something else. 'Whoa, is that a map of Ignisland?' He's pulled free from my grasp, moving towards another doorway, and I can see what he's looking at. On the wall, a huge map of Ignisland, the fictional land in *The Quest of Byron,* the same map that appears at the front of the book. Depicted in full on one of Liam's walls. He really is a fan of the series.

'Yeah.' Liam's eyes go from me to Gabe as he stands perched on his crutches, as though considering something, and he then jerks his head towards the doorway. 'You want to see?'

'Uh, no, that's-'

'Heck yeah,' Gabe says, scurrying into the room, leaving me hanging. Not knowing what else to do, I follow.

My jaw actually drops when I walk into the room. Like the hallway, the walls are wood-panelled, the dark floorboards waxed and covered in Persian carpets, a huge chandelier hanging from the high ceiling. There's a fireplace, flames roaring even though it's summer, in front of which are two leather armchairs. Half of the room, on my left, is nothing but books - some on shelves, some scattered across the floor, others piled high on what's probably supposed to be a dining table. I turn my head to the right, where Gabe saw the map, and realise that's not the only piece of memorabilia. This guy must be a *Quest of Byron* super fan, because there are dozens of copies of the books, pictures of the covers in frames, maps and drawings related to the story scattered everywhere. The only thing that stops this room from looking like something from centuries ago is the MacBook in the middle of the desk, the laptop open, Apple logo on the back lit up.

'Wow,' I say involuntarily.

Gabe has gone right up to the map hanging on the wall, and is looking at all the other pictures linked to the books, when he turns around with a grin on his face. 'You're W. J. Heathcote? Are you really? But how - *William*. Of course. Liam is short for William.'

'You're W. J. Heathcote?' I repeat.

Liam shrugs. 'Maybe.'

'That explains why there are so many of your books in the phone box library,' Gabe says.

Liam just shrugs again.

'It's funny,' Gabe goes on, 'because most people who write fantasy books look like wizards, and you don't.'

'Gabe!' I thump him on the arm, and he yelps.

'See,' Liam says, 'I don't know if I'm offended by that generalisation, or kind of upset you don't think I look like a wizard.'

The joke takes me by such surprise that I laugh, as does Gabe beside me. 'So you work from home,' I say. 'In this room. That's why you never leave the house.'

Liam frowns. 'I leave sometimes.'

'Not much,' Gabe says. 'We've been keeping tabs on you. We thought you were maybe a vampire, but this is *so* much cooler.'

'Um, thank you?'

'How did you break your leg?' I ask.

'Oh.' He thinks about this for a moment, as though there have been many broken legs and he's trying to figure out which one I'm referring to. 'I tripped over a pile of books.'

'So you're writing the fourth right now?' Gabe asks, creeping dangerously close to the computer screen.

'Yes, but...' Liam hesitates. 'It's not going so well. Driving me a bit mad, if I'm honest. That's why I've been home more than usual, and I'm spaced out all the time... I'm supposed to have it with my editor next month, but it's not looking likely.'

'You shouldn't have a problem, your books are great!' Gabe says. 'I'm sure anything you write will be amazing.'

'It's tricky, keeping track of everything that's happened and making sure I've resolved it all and not written myself into a corner.'

'If you need someone who knows everything that happens in the books, I can help! I remember everything.'

Liam looks interested. 'Really?'

'It's true,' I say. 'Gabe's got one of those photographic memories.'

Liam nods slowly. 'I might take you up on that. I hate reading back things I've already written...'

I leave them when I realise that Gabe shows no signs of coming home anytime soon, because I need to get to the yard to feed Jupiter. Even if now, walking back up the lane, earlier's events are rushing back to me, and I just want to hide in a hole in the ground and never come out.

Before going to the stables, I stop to tell Mum where Gabe is so she doesn't worry, and then hurry off before she can start asking too many questions, because the past ten minutes cannot be explained in few words.

chapter 9

'Hey, you okay?'

I saw her trailer when I arrived at the yard, and now Georgia stands in front of Jupiter's stable door, the girl who was here the first time I had a lesson. She's just ridden, her horse tied to the trailer after a jumping session, and she regards me with concern. So now Rose is telling people about my failures and setting them up to check on me? Why else would this person be in front of me now.

'Fine,' I say curtly, flicking my wrist to brush out Jupiter's sweat marks.

Georgia nods slowly but doesn't move. Jupiter puts his head over the door, seeing that he has an admirer, and she smiles at him, scratching his head. 'He's a sweetie,' she says. 'I wish I'd had a pony like him growing up.'

'What kind of pony did you have?' I ask.

'Oh, no, I didn't. Never had a pony. Didn't get a horse until I was some years older than you.'

'Oh,' I say. 'Did you ride though?'

She shakes her head. 'Not much. Probably started when

I was your age. My parents aren't horsey, and definitely couldn't afford to fund my want to ride, so I just had to work to afford it. I started exercising racehorses as soon as I was old enough, just to have the chance to ride.'

I nod like all this is trivial, but really my mind is running through the images of Georgia riding, remembering how she looked liked she'd been on a horse the better part of her life.

'Rose helped me out masses, too,' she says. 'Still does.'

'She's nice like that,' I say, keeping my eyes on Jupiter's coat, concentrating on getting out every last bit of dried sweat. As fit as he is, he now almost always has a triangle of sweat on his neck.

'Yeah, she is.' There's a moment of silence, and I wonder if Georgia's walked away, not wanting to look up and check, but then I know she hasn't because she goes on. 'You know, I always used to feel like I was fighting a losing battle. I had a family that couldn't tell an event horse from a donkey, no support system, not even a patch of land to keep a horse on. I wanted to be an event rider when I'd never even been around a cross country course. And then I'd see these other people the same age as me with bucketloads of experience, and nice horses and parents' money behind them… At least that's how it always looked. You know, people born into riding families, who'd never known what it's like to have to fight just to ride. And I'd think it was all so unfair, and that any of us could succeed if given the same opportunities, and that I deserved to do well just because I didn't have any of that, and that somehow the universe owed it to me. And at the risk of sounding preachy, I eventually realised that thinking like that was setting myself up for failure. But more than that, more than thinking I'd been dealt a bad card and that the odds were stacked against me, what I realised was how hard these people who seemed to have it easy actually had to work. Sure, there are some kids out there who get bought team horses and never have to lift a finger, only ride and never worry about where the money's coming from. But so many of them don't. I discovered that the people I thought had it easy actually worked for everything they had, harder than me, and never took anything for granted. They might have started off with an advantage, but they have to work to keep it, and by thinking that I deserved to triumph over them because I hadn't had the same opportunities I was just setting myself up to fail. And I also thought every setback was the end of the world, and that I was kidding myself, when really I was just making mistakes and learning, and things would have been so much easier if I hadn't got it into my head that I had it tough. I'm not saying I didn't work hard too, but there's a difference. You don't succeed because you *want* to. Sitting around and wishing you were good at something doesn't get you anywhere. The moment you start acting like the universe owes you something is the moment you set yourself up to fail. Anyway, the point is that at competitions, you see everyone's best. You see the result of hard work, but everyone fails behind closed doors. My friends who have been on European teams and have support systems behind them have still fallen just as many times, still faced disappointment, still get up before the sun every morning and work their butts off. Well, maybe not at the moment, because the sun *does* rise super early' - I laugh, trying to hold back involuntary tears - 'but they work just the same. And if they stopped working, eventually they'd fall behind. They might have better horses and set-ups and more natural talent, but in the long run that doesn't matter. Horses are fair that way. It doesn't matter where you're from, how early you start riding, or even how terrible you are to begin with, because you can work your way to the top. One step at a time. And that means tripping up every now and then.'

Jupiter's mane goes blurry as I stare at it, trying to keep my eyes as still as possible. I barely know this person standing in front of me, yet her words ring true, and it doesn't seem fair not to say something back when she's just opened up like that. 'I just always feel like I'm useless,' I croak.

'Me too. Half the time, I'm convinced I'm the worst event rider on the planet. But I know that I can change that. Riding ability can improve. What doesn't change is the love I feel for my horse, and the thrill I feel when I come off a cross country course, or even just nail a dressage movement. And if I really am useless, then so be it. At least I can say that I've done exactly what I wanted to with my life, and I won't look back in ten years' time and wonder what could have been if I'd stuck with it.' Georgia looks over her shoulder, at her horse tied to the trailer. 'I'd better go, because they'll all be wanting their dinner. I just...' Her voice trails off as she turns back to me. 'Bad days feel like the end of the world, and they really aren't. And I'm sure life doesn't feel fair, but you can work through every problem. Everyone else's success doesn't define yours. Wanting something isn't enough, you have to work for it. I... I just wanted to say to you what I wish somebody had told me.'

I wait until I hear the Jeep start and see the back of the trailer roll out of the yard, onto the road, before letting myself out of the stable. Rose is in the hay barn on the other side of the yard, and I hurry away before I get stuck in a conversation, to Ace's stable.

'Hey, Maggot,' I say quietly, unlatching the door. I never call her Maggot to anyone else, but unfortunately Freya is right. It does kind of suit her.

The mare lifts her pretty head from her hay, jaw moving as she grinds the strands. She regards me a moment, only to pin her ears and return to the forage. There's dried sweat where her numnah was, which I didn't sponge off earlier, and I feel guilt settle in my stomach.

'Let me get that off,' I say. I put her head collar on, because I never know when she'll try to bite while I'm grooming her, and start rubbing the sweat marks, keeping the lead rope in my left hand. Ace stands still, showing her disapproval in the way she doesn't relax. Unlike Jupiter, who would let you brush him all day.

'You're a funny one, you know that?' The mare turns her head to look at me, and I touch the perfect heart-shaped star between her eyes. 'Sorry I rode you so badly,' I say. 'I'm working on that. But I won't give up. Not if you let me keep going.'

Ace flickers an ears, then takes a step away to lower her nose to the water bucket. After a few seconds, she lifts her head again, regarding me, and then opens her mouth to let all the water she just inhaled fall to the ground, tongue sticking out as she mashes her jaw. Her ears are forward, and she stares at me, as if trying to work out if I find her party trick amusing. I laugh. 'Yes, okay you're funny.' She licks her lips some more, then touches her nose to my arm and licks me instead. It's not much, but it's the most affection she's ever shown me. 'I'll take that as a yes, then.' And then, because she's still Ace, she decides she's fed up of me, pins her ears, and returns to her hay. 'All right, I get it, you're scary.' But I'm smiling. Even if my pony switches from normal to evil in 2.4 seconds.

I keep going, every day. I ride Ace and I make mistakes and I learn from them. I listen to Rose and apply the corrections she tells me. When we jump, Ace still tries to take off on landing, but I learn to control it, and remember my voice. Ace responds to voice commands, and to my surprise, even when's she in a blind panic, it works.

We jump, and hack, and jump, and hack some more. There's no magic turning point, no breakthrough moment, just repetition. Pole exercises. Grids. Walking Ace in to fences and only trotting at the last moment, again and again until she stops taking off. I learn how she likes to be ridden, and we work together. I'm riding Jupiter at the same time, and between the two completely different ponies, I find my own riding improving. I learn different things from each, and apply those things to the other. Rose suggests that Ace is ready for some show jumping rounds, and we go to clear round show jumping evenings nearby, and while nothing is straightforward, and I still make mistakes and Ace is still tricky when she gets into a competition environment, we manage. I take Jupiter too, and he jumps so well his first time out since the disastrous event that I could burst with happiness. Everything feels like it's coming together, and even when it doesn't, I don't let myself get upset by it.

'I think it's time we take this girl cross country schooling,' Rose says one evening. 'She still needs to get around an event next month and be advertised.'

'How much is she worth, do you think?' I ask.

'Not sure. I don't think they'd let her go for less than a certain amount, but they can't exactly ask for loads for her. I don't want to say and be wrong, but if I got her round clear, I think they'd ask in the region of four and hope she goes to someone who can manage her.'

'Four thousand?' My mind boggles. I have that, just about, but it's a ridiculous amount to me, and I'm not sure Mum would be up for me spending my entire child support savings on a pony.

'Why?' Rose smiles. 'You interested in keeping the devil?'

I do my best to look like I don't care. 'Just curious.'

Jupiter and Ace are loaded onto the lorry a few days later, and Rose and I are heading to a cross country course on a nearby estate. Sheep roam free among the jumps, which Ace doesn't mind, but Jupiter is convinced they're going to eat him, and it's only after seeing how unbothered Ace is that he starts to relax.

I'm on Jupiter while Rose starts Ace off, the mare looking around unsurely. I trot Jupiter around, working him the same way I would in a school, keeping an eye on Ace as I do. She's really bulked up these past weeks, though still nowhere near Jupiter. Her dark coat dappled, muscles rippling with every stride, head carriage high and round. Rose is tall for her, but she still looks right, especially since, in her own words, Ace is more like a little horse than a pony.

After a shaky start, Ace raises the bar. Realising that Rose isn't going to hurt her or give her mixed signals, she starts jumping with more enthusiasm, and she jumps well. Really well. She tucks her knees and takes off boldly and swings over the fences with enough scope to make me think she could go all the way to FEI. I give Jupiter a little jump, too, and he feels great. He's always loved cross country, always been gung-ho, and he pulls me towards every fence, thrilled to be jumping natural obstacles.

Ace has a small tantrum at a ditch, but it's quickly sorted, and when Rose points her at a trakehner, a harder fence consisting of a ditch *and* a log above it, she jumps that no problem.

'Right, I've done what I need for the event,' Rose says once she trots the mare through the water. 'I'll take her over the ditch at home a few times before next weekend, but I'm pleased. Do you want a go?'

I'm nervous I'll do something to mess Ace up, but I do want to see what she's like cross country, and Rose holds both ponies while I get on, before getting on Jupiter herself. 'Armchair,' she says happily, letting her feet swing at his sides. I shorten my own stirrups a few holes, then get Ace going in a canter. She's moving with more purpose than she usually does, happy, like how she is on a hack, but also spicier. Once I have her going in a safe rhythm, Rose directs me to a fence, and I turn Ace to the simple log. She doesn't tank towards it the way Jupiter does, but stays in her rhythm, and Rose calls at me to keep the energy up, which I do, and Ace soars. She jumps bigger than Jupiter, but also more fluidly, and I'm grinning when we land clear the other side.

Rose directs me over some more fences, even some combinations, and Ace jumps everything. She's not as straightforward a ride as Jupiter, but she's also easier in a different way, because she doesn't do anything without being asked. I have to work harder to keep her straight over corners, and she won't jump the second part of a combination without me telling her to, but she's bold. And brave. Makes me feel like I could point her at that huge table over there and she'd fly over it effortlessly.

'I don't know about you,' Rose says to me in the lorry on the way home, 'but I think that was a success.'

The early morning sunshine that promises a hot day doesn't lie, and the weather is glorious at the event. The sunlight makes Ace gleam as Rose trots her around the warm-up ring. She's been calm since arriving, and looks it now as she works her way around the other horses.

'Hi Sybil,' says Nell, coming up to me. Her clothes are simple, as always, and long curls of hair escape from their bun. There's a rucksack over her shoulder, and she's carrying a dressage whip and a small bottle of water. 'How are you doing? Is Rose riding?'

I nod. 'She's on Ace.'

Nell picks the mare out of the warm-up and looks impressed. 'Wow, she's looking amazing! So what's happening with her next? Is she being sold?'

'Supposed to be,' I say cautiously. 'She still has her quirks, though.'

'Well, I'm sure everything will work out.'

'Leo's looking good,' I say. It's Freya's first event with the pony, but you wouldn't tell looking at them. The chestnut gelding is moving around the ring with elegance, perfectly balanced and collected, Freya looking just as professional. She looks like she's been riding him forever.

'He's a honey,' Nell says. 'I think Freya's quite nervous, though.'

'She doesn't look it,' I comment. She looks serious and concentrated, as she always does, but not nervous.

'Hmm.' Nell doesn't look convinced. 'I don't know, we'll see. I'd better go check she's all right. Good luck.'

'You too.'

Rose starts working Ace in canter, the mare containing her energy and overflowing with class, and when she comes to a trot and a walk, she's heading for a few people standing on the edge of the warm-up, halting beside them. As they exchange greetings and start fussing over Ace, I realise who it must be: her owners. A typical wealthy country woman in her fifties, a tag along husband, and the daughter who must have been Ace's rider before. They don't look horrid, far from it, but I feel a chill, seeing them stroke Ace and gush over her. Weird to think she's more their horse than anyone else's.

The bay mare puts in a good test, if a little tense, but her owners seem very happy when she comes out. Freya was in a different ring at the same time, quite a few spectators openly staring at the chestnut pony as he executed the movements, and I'll be shocked if she isn't in the top five after that.

Sunny and Paddington are here too, and I stay with Ace while Rose rides her other dressage tests, walking her around and holding her for grass. I get her ready for show jumping before Rose is due back, and then lead her to the warm-up ring. It isn't long until her rider is heading this way, carrying a whip, saying hello to most of the people she passes, both two and four-legged. She says, 'Hi Zach,' to one person and then bends to the greyhound he has on a lead and says, 'Hello Lily,' with just as much care. And she seems to know everyone.

'Thank you for getting her ready,' she says to me, pulling down Ace's stirrups.

'No problem. So were those her owners at the dressage?'

'Yep. Celeste, she's called. Very nice.'

'Were they happy? What did they think of her?'

'Oh, they're thrilled. They think she looks fab. And she does. Let's just see if we still think that after the jumping phases.'

Rose gets Ace on a good stride every jump of the warm-up, and she couldn't be in better shape to tackle the course as they enter the ring.

'Next to jump will be number 537 Rose Holloway and Ace of Hearts, riding for Mrs Celeste Matthews.'

The start bell goes, and Rose pushes Ace into a canter. The mare rushes forward, tucking her nose to her chest, but Rose steadies her, bringing her up off the forehand. I hold my breath almost the whole way around, only letting it out once when Ace rushes into the combination and takes the first rail, but Rose gets her back in time for the second part, and the rest of the round is faultless.

'One down for Rose Holloway and Ace of Hearts, adding four faults to their dressage score of 33.4, meaning they go into cross country on a score of 37.4.'

'Unlucky,' I tell Rose as I jog to her side, patting Ace's neck. 'The rest was really good.'

'The rail was my fault, anyway,' Rose says. 'I felt her running away, but I didn't want to take a pull.'

I'm a nervous wreck at the cross country warm-up, probably looking how Mum does whenever I'm about to ride. Ace's plaits have been pulled out and her mane is in tight curls along the crest of her neck.

'Three, two, one, go! Good luck!'

Ace shoots out of the start box, Rose standing in her stirrups and urging her on, and they soar over the first fence, galloping to the next.

I run around the course, trying to see as much of the round as I can. My heart is in my mouth as I watch Ace go around, even as it occurs to me that it could work to my advantage if she didn't go well and subsequently weren't worth as much, but I can't hope for that. Rose and I have put in too much time for me to want anything to go wrong, and Ace doesn't deserve that.

I manage to make it back to the last fence in time to see Ace clear it, and Rose pats her neck on landing as they carry on to the finish flags. Clear round.

'You did it,' I yell, running to Rose's side as she trots the pony on a circle beyond the finish, letting her catch her breath slowly.

'She was great,' Rose says, only blowing a little herself. 'Way more switched on than the other day. A real cross country machine.'

I wrap my arms around Ace's neck, and she doesn't even pin her ears. 'Super girl,' I tell her.

'Rose, that was fantastic!' comes a woman's voice, and I know it's Ace's owner before I even turn around. She has the face of someone who's spent many years outside, worn and weathered, her hair immaculately blow-dried. She must have ditched her family, because they aren't around. 'I didn't think you'd get Maggot going as well as that.'

'She's not so much of a Maggot,' Rose says with a smile. 'Celeste, this is Sybil, who's been a big help with the mare. She's more the right size for her, so she's been riding her a lot for me at home.'

'Hello,' Celeste says warmly. 'Well, you've both done a great job, anyhow. And hopefully I'll have her out of your hair very soon after that.'

I look away, blood running cold at those words.

'She's still not that straightforward,' Rose says cautiously. 'I wouldn't be comfortable passing her on to any kid.'

'I know, she gets strong,' Celeste says, and I want to scream *No, she doesn't. She doesn't get strong, she just takes off when she's scared.* 'But I actually have someone in mind. You know the Bensons? One of their sons is looking for another pony. He's a big chap, so I figured he'd have no problem keeping her under control.'

The thought of some thug-like boy sitting on Ace makes me want to cry, and I run a hand down her neck.

'Just before you get into that,' Rose says, 'what are you asking for her?'

'Well, I'm not exactly going to give her away, and you and I know how much event ponies are these days. She had some good results before, and she still has plenty of time to get more. I'm thinking six or seven.'

Seven thousand! For Ace?

Rose looks at me. 'Sybil has put a lot of work into her, and she and Maggot really get on, and I think she was maybe interested in taking her off your hands.' I've never said that to Rose, not in so many words, but it doesn't matter, because she knows that's what I've been thinking, and is confident to say it out loud without me confirming it.

'Really?' Celeste looks excited. 'Oh, well that would be even better.'

'I can't quite say for sure yet,' I tell her. 'But my mum is open to it. Though I don't quite have that much,' I admit.

Celeste looks at Ace. 'Well, at the end of the day, I want her to have a nice home. And as you've already been working her yourself, I guess I could make an exception. And of course I trust you, Rose, implicitly.'

'Can we get back to you in a few days?' says Rose. 'I

know Sybil's mum well and I can vouch for her intent, but it's still something that needs to be discussed a little more.'

'Of course, of course. Take as long as you need, just let me know.'

Once Ace and Jupiter are tucked in their stables with hay and feed, Ace with her legs wrapped, I run the whole way home. I'm too excited, desperate to tell Mum about meeting Celeste and see if I really can spend my child support savings on Ace. I still find her annoying half the time, and she frequently bites me, and fusses, and is more trouble than she's worth, but I've also found myself falling for her. Some weeks ago, I'd have been only too happy to see the back of her. Now nothing could be further from the truth.

Mum's back is turned when I come crashing into the cottage. 'How was it?' she asks.

'It was amazing! Ace was amazing, and she did so well, even if she didn't place. Oh, and Freya and Leo came second by the way. Anyway, back to Ace, she was just so so incredible, and her owners were there, and the woman was really nice, and she wanted six or seven for her, but she said since I've been working her I could have her for less because she just wants her to go to a good home, and can I? I know we've talked about it, but can I really? I'll cover all her costs myself, I swear. And Jupiter's. I'll work in the café and help Rose and even find other work, I don't know, but I will. I promise. I'll find a way.' I pause to take a breath, chest heaving from the rambling. 'Please, Mum? Can I get her?'

Mum has been facing the other way this whole time, and she slowly turns to me, her face wearing an expression that makes the bottom drop out of my stomach.

'What's happened?' I ask, and I realise someone's missing. 'Is Gabe okay?'

'Gabe's fine, he's at Liam's. It's nothing like that,' Mum reassures me.

'Then what is it?' I almost don't want to know, premonition that whatever it is is about to ruin everything. But everyone's fine, and I know the horses are all fine because I've just left them, so I have no idea what else it could be.

I hear Mum's sharp intake of breath. 'Johanna called today.'

'Johanna Atkinson?' I ask. 'Jupiter's owners?'

Mum nods. 'Yeah. They've come into some tough times, and they're selling up everything they can to get cash.' Mum pauses, and I now know what she's going to say, as much as I wish I didn't. 'They're selling everything they can,' she repeats. 'Jupiter's for sale.'

chapter 10

I stare at the photograph propped up on the shelves in the kitchen. Jupiter, at an event last year, jumping a brush fence, me in my cross country colours of navy blue and white. It was raining that day, and the sky behind us is grey, the ground muddy. Looking at the picture now, knowing more than I did back then, I can pick out faults. Like how Jupiter's front legs aren't tidy, how we've taken off too far away, and how my body isn't forward enough, legs too far back. But Jupiter is still amazing. I say jump, he says how high? It didn't matter that I was riding badly, and that he was unfit and probably stiff then too. He jumped. Always does. Gives his all for me.

'It's not fair,' I manage, wrapping my hands around the mug of tea. Despite my change of attitude recently, resolution to stop feeling sorry for myself, it's the only thing I can think to say.

'I know,' Mum says. 'I know. It isn't fair.'

I state the facts out loud again. 'Jupiter's for sale, Ace is for sale, there's no way I can afford them both. And I've spent all summer working to get Jupiter right. And earning Ace's trust.'

'Johanna's given us first refusal, but we have to let her know soon.'

Tears fall down my face again, one landing in my tea. 'Just when I think everything's going well, something always goes wrong.'

'I know.' Mum gets up from her seat and wraps an arm around my shoulders. 'I know. But this is outside of our control. You know if I could get both...' Her voice drifts as she shakes her head. 'I just don't have it.'

'I know.'

'Sleep on it. But Johanna wants an answer, so we're going to have to decide soon.'

Exhaustion catches up with me, because somehow I sleep, reality waking me up at six the next morning. Everything looks better in the morning, that's what Mum always says, but the rule doesn't apply to this. This definitely doesn't look any better.

I pull clothes on and creep down the stairs, past the sleeping dogs, push my feet into boots, and head out the door. It's already been light for hours, and the sun shines directly into my eyes, a sharp contrast to my mood.

The yard is quiet. Rose feeds after seven, which means she won't be out for an hour yet. I go to Ace's stable first, only to tiptoe away just as quickly when I see her lying down over the half door, and then head for Jupi. He is also lying down, but unlike Ace, I know he won't be startled by my presence.

'Hey, Jup,' I say, letting myself in the stable. The grey pony barely moves, bottom lip hanging the way it does when he's asleep. I feel tears coming on again, but I hold them back determinedly, sitting beside the pony. I run my hand down his neck, his silky summer coat, and thread my fingers through his thick, silver mane. Jupiter closes his eyes, and I lean into him. This summer, I've been prepared for losing Ace, but not Jupiter. Never Jupiter. Even though he isn't much to look at, just another grey Connie on the eventing circuit, and not the biggest jumper, or the best dressage horse. But he's special. He's looked after me, taken me around my first tracks, taught me. Maybe that's all schoolmasters do, pass from one beginner to the next, making up for mistakes, never getting the chance to shine. And unless I pass him on, I'll never get the chance to ride a pony like Ace. But then…

Jupiter sighs loudly, lowering his head.

But then I'd just be doing what everyone else does. I'll be no better than Freya, abandoning the pony I swore I'd never give up just so that I can move on to something better. I don't want to be like that. I don't want to be one of those riders. And Rose did say, during our first lesson, that she thought Jupiter could go one-star.

But Ace. I can't imagine Ace with anyone else. She's only just started to trust everyone here, to trust *me,* and now we're going to break that by shipping her off, getting rid of her the way the Matthewses have. Just when she was starting to be understood. Jupiter could manage somewhere else, Ace couldn't.

'I'll be back in a minute,' I tell Jupiter, straightening up.

I walk to Ace's stable again, where she is now standing. Her head is over the door, and I go right up to her, but she pins her ears, threatening to bite, and I take a step back. 'And here I am crying over you,' I tell her, not able to feel any anger towards the mare as much as I wish I could. That would make things so much easier.

Ace pricks her ears again, and I think she's going to be friendly, but her eyes are fixed on something in the distance, and I follow her gaze to see a pony being ridden this way. Cinder, and Mackenzie, coming up from the grass riding paddock. I check my watch, sure it must be later than I thought, but it's not even half past six.

'Morning,' Mackenzie says brightly, bare-armed and red in the face as she rides the bay mare over.

Despite my mood, I almost laugh at her cheerful disposition. 'Morning,' I say back. 'You're up early.'

'Because it's so bright. I always wake up when the sun does, and all I want to do is ride.'

I nod. 'Makes sense.'

'Are you riding?' Mackenzie asks, walking Cinder to her stable with her feet out of the stirrups, sliding off her back only once they reach the half door. The horse in the stable next to Cinder, a bay called Brumby whose owner, Rose has told me, is heading to Cambridge on a full scholarship next month, stretches his nose to say hello to the mare.

'Uh, no, I don't think so. I just couldn't sleep, either.'

She runs up her stirrups and leads Cinder into the stable. 'So are you going to buy Ace?'

One thing to be said about kids is that they don't beat around the bush. 'I don't know.'

'Mum said you might be.'

'I know, but things have got complicated.'

Mackenzie swings her saddle over the half door. 'Why?'

I sigh. 'You know how Jupiter belongs to someone else, and she lends him to me?'

Mackenzie nods.

'Well, she called yesterday to say she's selling him.'

Mackenzie's face falls. 'Jupiter's going?'

'I don't know,' I tell her. 'I can buy him-'

'Yes, you have to buy him!'

'-but if I do that, I can't afford to buy Ace.'

'You can have my money!' Mackenzie says. 'I have forty-seven pounds, will that help?'

I pull a face. 'Not unless you can add a couple of zeros on to the end. Thank you, anyway.'

'What are you going to do, then?'

'I don't know. I guess I have to choose, and one will have to be sold.'

Mackenzie looks thoughtful. 'Mum sold a horse once.'

'I'm sure she's sold a few,' I say.

'No, but she sold one she didn't want to sell,' Mackenzie says, expression set as she goes on. 'A long time ago, before I was born, she had an amazing grey horse called Orion, and she loved him more than anything.'

'And what happened?'

'Someone made her an offer she couldn't refuse,' Mackenzie recites. 'He's been around Badminton now and everything. And Mum doesn't know I know this, but she still cries when she looks at pictures of him.'

My heart contracts, and I wonder what Mackenzie's point is, other than making me feel worse. 'Okay...'

'And when I ask her why she sold him, she says she had to give him up in order to have the life she has now. The money she got for him paid for the deposit on the yard,' Mackenzie says, sounding older than she is. 'So even though it was hard, she had to give up one thing in order to have another.'

'That's really sad.'

'Yes, but it's okay. Because sometimes you have to give something up.'

I do go for a ride eventually. Jupiter wasn't worked yesterday, so he's the one who needs to get out, and I tack him up as soon as an hour passes since he was fed. He's great to hack out alone now, walking calmly and never spooking. He never had any reason not to be, it was only my fault for not taking him out enough.

There are few cars on the road, and I don't pass any other horses on the bridleways. Jupiter walks steadily on a loose rein, ears forward, mane bobbing up and down with his stride. I lean forward to wrap my arms around his neck. 'You're the best,' I tell him. 'You really are.' But then my thoughts drift to Ace, the anxious little mare, and the way she sometimes looks so hopeful, even when she might have just bitten me a moment before, and my heart breaks. Will anyone else understand her? I can just imagine her being thrown into another yard, scared and confused, and falling back into the same place she was when she got here.

As we come back to the road, I've almost made a U turn in my mind. No one else will understand Ace, she'll be miserable, but Jupiter will survive. He'll go to a better home, take better care of himself.

But then I see Willow Tree House. The thatch roof, the white walls, the huge willow tree. And past it, I see a paddock that used to be home to a spotted pony. Except there isn't a spotted pony there anymore, but a flashy chestnut with European medals to his name. How is me giving up Jupiter for another pony any different from what Freya's done? Even if there's possibly more to that story, she gave up her ordinary pony for one that will win ribbons.

Something I swore I'd never do.

I turn Jupiter out at full speed, throwing my saddle and bridle in the tack room, and run home as quickly as I can, ignoring the stable that needs to be mucked out. It's eight o'clock, I should just catch Mum before she leaves for work...

'Hey, sweetie, I'm just on my way out.' Mum stands with her handbag over one shoulder and her car keys in her hand. 'Are you okay?'

I nod, tears clouding my vision again. Why can't I stop crying? 'I can't give Jupiter up,' I sob. 'I'm so scared for Ace, and Jupiter might do better with someone else, but...' I wipe my eyes. 'I can't give him up. I couldn't live with myself. I can't give him up the way Freya did Diamond.'

School isn't far away, and I spend every moment I can at the yard. With Ace too, not only Jupiter. It makes me feel even guiltier, but I'd feel worse if I just went on ignoring her. None of this is her fault.

'Someone's coming to try Ace tomorrow,' Rose tells me one evening while I'm mixing feeds. 'First thing.'

'Okay.'

'Would you be here? To get her ready and ride her?'

My blood feels like it's burning my skin, singeing it beneath the surface, but I nod. 'Sure.'

'Great. Thank you so much. I'll see you then.'

I don't sleep at all, tossing and turning, wondering what these people will be like, and resolve to sabotage everything if I decide they aren't worthy of Ace. That makes me feel slightly better, and I almost drift off to a sound sleep, but then my alarm clock is going, telling me it's time to get up.

'I'll come with you,' Mum announces at breakfast. 'I

don't have to be at the café yet, so I can be there for moral support.'

Despite me telling her not to bother, Mum insists, and we both get to the yard at seven. Rose has already fed, and I start grooming Ace as she pulls at her haylage, making her shine. Pick out and oil her feet, comb her tail. It's when I start getting her tack that the reality hits me, and my eyes start swimming again. But I keep going, push through it, until there's nothing to do but wait.

'What time did they say they'd be here?' I ask Rose, standing with Mum outside the stable.

'Quarter to eight,' she says.

I look at my watch. 'It's already gone eight.'

Rose looks down at her own watch. 'Huh.' She looks up at me and Mum, a clueless expression on her face. 'You're right. Maya, it's gone eight.'

'So it has,' Mum says.

'Do you think they're not going to show?' I ask.

Rose ignores me, still looking at Mum. 'I guess she'd better get on her, then.'

I stare at them both, trying to understand what they're saying, and as their faces break into grins, I shake my head. I don't want to hope, don't want to imagine. 'What're you talking about?'

'Well,' Rose says, 'aren't you going to try her?'

'What?'

'Don't look at me,' Mum says. 'This is all Rose.'

'What're you talking about?'

'She's yours,' Rose says.

'Is this a joke?' I say, looking from one face to the other.

'No,' Mum says, almost crying. 'Ace isn't going anywhere. Rose arranged everything. She's yours. Though

I've insisted Rose own her on paper.'

'You bought her?' I say. I didn't think Rose had that kind of money lying around, let alone to spend on a pony for somebody else.

'Not exactly. I just let all the schooling and livery costs go. Comes to about the same, and Celeste was more than happy with the arrangement. I did warn you I'm no businesswoman.'

'I can't believe it.'

'Don't just stand there,' Mum says. 'Give the woman a hug.'

I do throw my arms around Rose, only briefly because I'm still in too much shock.

'Go on,' Rose says. 'Take that pony of yours for a ride.'

I turn back to Ace, standing tacked up in the stable, my limbs shaking. I used to dread riding her, but right now there's nothing else I'd rather do.

chapter 11

This time, I'm the one riding Ace at the next event. I was going to ride Jupiter too, but he got balloted out. Besides, it's probably better that I only have one horse to think about today.

Ace is excited, like riding a pogo stick, and I'm a ball of nerves as we head to the dressage warm-up. But even as she spooks and leaps about, nothing like she was with Rose, I can't help but smile knowing this pony is mine to ride.

With Rose's help, I manage to gain some control of the mare during the warm-up. But when the steward calls our number, directing me to the dressage arena, I lose all sense of cool, and Ace feels it. Our test is a disaster, but by some miracle we stay within the white boards and execute each movement after a fashion.

I'm disappointed, feeling like I've already messed up the day, but Mum pulls me aside before tacking up for show jumping.

'No sulking,' she says firmly. 'Remember you're lucky to have this pony at all, and I won't have you moping about because of a bad score.'

Ace is feisty in the show jumping warm-up, and I make the mistake of trying to hold her back. This only makes her more irritated, and we manage to get over the fences somehow, though it's probably not pretty.

'You happy to go in?' Rose asks, unsure.

I nod.

'Next on course is number 589 Sybil Dawson, riding Mrs Rose Holloway's Ace of Hearts.'

The bell goes, and with it my head. Suddenly I can't think straight. The jumps are too big, too bright, the horse beneath me too strong and too fast. I almost freeze, except that in my stage fright panic, I pull.

Ace speeds away, tanking towards the fence, and I try to hold her back, get some sort of control. The closer we get to the first fence, the more I realise I have no stride. There's no short or long option. There's nothing. And yet I still try to go, but Ace isn't having it.

She almost takes off, starts to, then realises there's no way she can get over it, and slams on the brakes, too late for me to react. I go flying over her head, falling into the parallel of poles, and Ace pulls back as the bell rings.

'Sadly that is an elimination for Sybil Dawson and Ace of Hearts, but luckily both horse and rider are on their feet and looking no worse for wear. Please remember you'll need to be checked out by a medic before you leave, and before getting on any other rides.'

Rose has jumped into the ring to catch Ace, which she manages with more ease than the last time I fell off. I fight back tears of disappointment and humiliation as I make my way over to them, watching Rose straighten out the tack.

'You okay?' she asks.

I nod. 'It was my fault,' I say bitterly.

'Yep, but you live and learn.' Rose looks at Mum, who has come up beside us. 'My first event, I fell four times in the warm-up, and then at the third fence on course. Maya?'

Mum nods. 'My first event was a disaster. I made it through show jumping, but I couldn't get my pony to leave the cross country start box.'

'This isn't *my* first event,' I point out.

Rose lifts her shoulders. 'It's your first with this pony. Now get back on quickly to jump a practice fence before somebody drags you off to the ambulance.'

I do as Rose says, climbing back onto Ace's back, Mum watching nervously from the sidelines, but I find that I'm not nervous anymore. It was the competition atmosphere that got to me, pressure I put on myself, and that's all gone now.

Ace jumps two warm-up fences perfectly, and Rose tells me to call it a day. I get off, pat the mare, and hand the reins to Mum to go off and see a medic as the stewards are hassling me to do. The ambulance is on one side of the show jumping ring, not far, and as I walk up to it, I can hear two voices inside it, loud and clear.

'For goodness' sake, I'm fine,' a girl is saying. 'I'm talking, aren't I?'

'I'm sure you'd still be talking even if your head were split in two, Ms Evans. You're also bleeding.'

I step opposite the ambulance to see a girl older than I expected - one of those faces that could be anywhere between fifteen and thirty, but I reckon early twenties - sitting on the stretcher, next to a paramedic. Her crash cap is beside her, and the navy blue silk that covers it embellished with a Union Jack. Whoever she is, she's been in a British squad. She does look slightly familiar, but I can't place her. Did he say Evans...

The girl looks down at her arm, at the trickle of blood. 'Well, obviously. I scraped my arm on the fence. Gee, if only there were such a thing as a plaster.'

'Ms Evans,' the paramedic warns.

'Well can you get a move on then?' she snaps, but it comes across as humorous rather than mean. 'I've got three more to ride today, including a cross country in ten minutes.'

'I'm just waiting for the other medic to get back.'

'Oh for the love of-'

'ALEX!' a voice beside me yells, and I turn to see a girl of similar age, but with a kinder face, dressed in white jodhpurs and a shirt, wearing the relaxed expression of someone who has finished riding for the day. 'Your mum sent me to see what you're up to.'

'Ask this buffoon,' she huffs, nodding at the paramedic.

'I'm very sorry for Alex's behaviour,' the girl says. 'You can gag her if she really gets on your nerves.'

'I might just do that.'

'Just tell her I'll be there in a sec, Leni,' Alex says. 'And you could always be a really nice friend and start warming Waffles up for me.'

Leni. Alex Evans. The names click in my mind, and I realise who these two girls are: Leo and Otto's former respective riders. The horse world is a small world, I remind myself.

'All the money in the world couldn't make me get on that thing,' Leni replies. 'And I'm only helping you out of the goodness of my heart. Anyway, I'll tell your mum you're on your way.'

'Uh-huh.' Alex sighs, looking down at her bleeding arm

again, which seems to be getting worse. She sounds young when she speaks, but she looks much older. Face bony, eyes serious, hair the length almost all mums you see at school pick-up wear theirs. 'Why are we waiting for the other medic again?' she asks the one beside her.

'I'm out of compresses.'

'Is that a joke? What if this were a serious matter of life or death?' Her eyes find me, standing in front of the ambulance. 'What about this girl?' she says. 'I don't think she's here because it's a cool place to hang out. Then again, I'm here, so maybe it is.'

I'm starting to see why India's parents find this girl rude.

'Can I help you?' the medic asks.

'Um, I just fell off, and they told me to come here,' I say. 'I feel fine.'

He nods. 'Okay. Do you-' His voice is cut off by a clatter of poles in the ring, the sound of hoofbeats, and somebody calling for a medic. 'I'll be right back.'

'Don't worry, it's not like we have anywhere to be,' Alex says. 'Oh, wait.'

'The other medic should be back any moment,' he says, hurrying away before Alex can say anything else.

'Well this is just great,' she says. She looks at me. 'Are you okay?'

I nod. 'Just fell off show jumping. It was my fault, but my mare's a bit difficult.'

'Hah, mares.' She laughs. 'You know, I used to hate mares, avoided them like the plague, then I fell for my mare and she's the greatest thing ever, and now I think they're awesome. Not that they're always easy.'

'Mares are cats, geldings are dogs,' I mutter.

'Sorry?'

'It's just something my trainer says. Mares are like cats, geldings are like dogs.'

'Oh, I like that. That's cool. Mares are cats, geldings are dogs. I'm going to use that. So how did you fall?'

'At the first fence,' I admit, embarrassed, and Alex laughs.

'That's awesome.' *Not the word I'd use.* 'I know it won't feel like it now,' she goes on, with more sincerity than I'd have thought her capable of, 'but trust me, you'll laugh too in a few years' time. All you can do when things go wrong is laugh. That's my motto, anyway. And drink tea, of course. Like today,' she continues, 'my horse - ditch-hating horse, granted - who has been round Badminton and jumped the Vicarage Vee just had a refusal at an Open Intermediate trakehner and sent me flying into the fence, and if I didn't laugh, I couldn't keep doing what I do.'

Just laugh. It seems as good advice as any, and we laugh together.

'Hey Maggot.'

Ace is tied to the lorry, pulling at her haynet, no worse for wear after our fall. I give her a hug, reminding myself how lucky I am just to have her. Today hasn't gone well, but there'll be other days. Ace isn't easy. I'm still learning. And this will be a funny story one day.

'Let's just try not to repeat this,' I tell the mare.

She pins her ears at me, swishing her tail and stomping her foot. I smile at her, not letting myself be fazed by her attitude, and slowly the temper fades as she returns to her hay. A good mare is better than any gelding, everyone says. If I get Ace on side, if she channels her character in the right direction, she could be extraordinary. A few months ago, it seemed as though my eventing season was doomed, but suddenly I have two prospects, two ponies to finish the season on and prepare for next year.

'What do you say, Maggot?' I ask, tilting my head to look her in the eye. 'Future FEI pony. You game?'

about the author

After years of living in France, Grace currently resides near Newmarket, where she works with horses full-time.

https://www.facebook.com/GraceWilkinsonWrites

gracewilkinsonwrites@gmail.com

Printed in Great Britain
by Amazon